Legacy

Ralph Nelson Willett

Proofreading provided by Mark Schultz, you can find him at
www.wordrefiner.com

Can I Ask A Favor?

If you enjoy this book, please consider providing a review on Amazon for it. Reviews help readers decide if they would like to purchase a book or not and is useful for the author when making decisions on what to write for his next book.

Here's the link where you can add your review:
www.NorthernOvationMedia.com/thelegacy/review

Thank you.

Want Free Books?

From time to time the author offers his Kindle books for free to those who are interested. <u>These offers are highly temporary.</u> If you'd like to know when you can get his books for free, please sign up for his mailing list at:
www.NorthernOvationMedia.com/freebooks

Chapter 1

Dear Jamie,
Would you like to know about your father?

Jamie Fulton stared at the first line of the hand-written note. As she read it, she could not know how this single sentence would suddenly and painfully complicate her life, culminating in the murder of a brother she had never known.

She read the rest of the brief note.

I'd love to tell you about him. If you're interested, you can meet me at this address anytime.

478 Main St.
Amison, Ohio

Brett St. James

The letter, written on brown stationery designed to appear antique, had a strong scent of men's cologne. The first page contained only a brief handwritten note in blue ink, block lettering.

She held the first page beneath her nose and sniffed its scent as she examined the second page. It was a picture of a church, skillfully drawn in pencil. The brick church was centered on a landscape of hills and trees. It had an enclosed bell tower on one corner that rose several feet above its roof. A grassy hill rose high behind it. At the top of the hill was a solitary tree in its center and to its right, leaning away from the tree was a cross. Behind the cross the sun appeared to be highlighting both the cross and the tree, giving them a haloed appearance.

She raised the drawing to her nose and sniffed the cologne again as she reread the note twice. She turned her unfocused gaze out of her kitchen window as she tried to place the name, Brett St. James. There was no one she could recall by that name.

Turning the pages over, she checked the back of each one for any further clues. So many questions came to mind. Someone was offering to tell her about her father. Why? How did Brett St. James know who her father was? What was the meaning of the picture of the church? It all touched the one question that had burned in her since she was a little girl: Who is my father?

She checked the drawing closely and rubbed her thumb over it. It smudged beneath her touch proving to her that it was an original sketch.

Again, she reread the note. She had lived in Ohio her entire life but had never heard of Amison. Pulling out her cell phone, she brought up Google Maps and entered the address. Amison was a rural community on the far side of Columbus from her home. Total drive time was about an hour and forty-five minutes. She could be there and back in an afternoon.

She pulled up Google Street View. The Street View photos of the church were a near perfect match with the pencil drawing. It was beautiful, with high stained-glass windows and large white front doors. It stood back from the street several yards with a wide sidewalk that began at the street and ended at the front steps. To the right of the church was a small cemetery, bordered by a knee-high wrought-iron fence. The headstones appeared to be old and weatherworn. The hill that rose behind the church was covered with wild grasses. The single tree appeared at the top as it had in the drawing. The only thing missing on the hill, that was shown in the drawing, was the cross.

Jamie carried the letter and her phone with her into the living room and sat on the sofa. She curled her feet up on the cushion, held the letter with two hands and read it again as if there was some secret meaning that only reading it repeatedly would reveal.

Her tabby cat leapt to the sofa and nuzzled against her arm. It tucked its head under her arm and glided up her chest until its nose reached her lips. It began to purr.

"What are you doing, sweetie?" Jamie asked as she stroked it gently with her free hand. The cat pushed its nose against her lips, causing Jamie to laugh and turn her head. "OK, OK," Jamie said as she chuckled. The cat settled into her lap expecting to have Jamie's full attention.

Jamie set the letter on the sofa armrest and used both hands to pet the cat. She stared down at the letter and read it again as she casually stroked her pet. She studied the picture again and tried to imagine what the church had to do with a father she had never known. Was he a priest? Was he a pastor? Was there some secret confession that could only be revealed now by his confessor? How was he connected to this church?

She had been raised as an only child in a single parent home. She had asked about him several times, but her mother had refused to tell her anything about him. Even on her birth certificate the space for the father had been left blank. The only related men that she had ever known was her grandfather and two uncles. Her father was never mentioned.

She mindlessly petted the tabby as her eyes glazed over in thought. She was thirty years old. Did she really want to know who her father was? She knew nothing about him. As far as she knew, only her mother knew anything about him. What was it about him that would cause her mother to keep him a secret all these years? Was he a man who would abandon his pregnant girlfriend? Was there something sinister about him? She had no answers. The cat turned on its back and allowed Jamie to scratch its belly as her mind wandered. "Who are you, Brett St. James?" She asked aloud.

~~~~~

All her waking moments seemed to have been focused on the letter since she first read it four days earlier. She left the letter unfolded and spread out on the kitchen island.

The Legacy

Several times she sat on the tall stool, reread it and examined the drawing again.

Did she really want to know about her father, she wondered? Why had her mother always refused to tell her anything about him? What dark secret would be revealed if she met him? Twice she had woken up restlessly in the middle of the night as the invitation to Amison tempted her.

She must have read the note fifty times, but reread it again as she sat and ate her dinner at the kitchen island. She finished her salad, folded the letter and set it on the counter top. Visions of the church floated through her mind as she placed her dishes in the dishwasher and closed the door. Taking a glass of water with her, she moved to the living room sofa and stared out of the front window as she let her mind wander. The church seemed to beckon her, calling out to her gently with the tease of finally knowing who her father was.

Brett St. James had not provided a telephone number. She had attempted to find one but there was no listing for him. Knowing something about her father, anything at all, was something that she had always wanted. Her curiosity pulled at her heavily, begging her to make the drive to Amison. If there was any chance that she could learn anything at all about him, the trip would be worth it.

She let out a heavy sigh, opened her cell phone and called her mother. It had been a long time since she had asked her mother anything about her father. She hoped enough time would have passed that her mother would feel free to tell her but, in reality, Jamie knew what to expect.

"Hi," her mother answered.

"Hi, Mom. What are you up to?"

"Dinner. What are you doing? Coming over this Sunday after church?"

"Yeah, but I need to ask you something," Jamie replied.

"What's up?"

Jamie hesitated, took a deep breath and asked, "Would you please tell me who my father is?"

The phone was silent.

"Mom?" Jamie prompted.

The pause continued a moment longer before her mother answered. "Jamie," she said and paused again, "I'm sorry. I can't."

"Mom," Jamie protested, "I'm not fourteen anymore. I'm not even eighteen. I think I can handle the truth even if it isn't good."

"I'm sorry, Jamie. I wish I could. I just can't."

"What if it's something that I really need to know?" Jamie asked. "What if there was something in my genetics that was passed down from my biological father? Wouldn't you want to know that?"

Another long pause. "Why are you asking about him now?" her mother asked her.

The Legacy

"I just gave you a reason," Jamie said, trying to conceal her frustration.

"Jamie, you're just going to have to trust me on this," her mother said. "It's something that I just can't share. Besides, it's been thirty years. What makes you think I can remember that far back?"

"Mom," Jamie said, "you can't give me that. You remember everything about everything."

"Jamie, what's making you ask about him now?"

Jamie hesitated. She did not want to tell her mother about the letter yet. If she told her, she may try to talk her out of going to Amison. "I've just been thinking about him a lot recently. Who was he? Do I have any siblings? Maybe a sister. Why are you hiding this from me?"

"Jamie, you have to trust me on this. There's nothing about your biological father that you need to know. That was something that happened a long time ago. Having you may have been the best thing I could have ever asked for, but it's not something I want to relive, and I have to ask you not to bring it up."

"Is the secret so dark?" Jamie asked.

"It's just a secret, Jamie. I made a promise that I would never tell anyone. It's just a secret, but I'm afraid that I'm going to take this to my grave. You'll be much happier not knowing anything about him. Trust me." Jamie was quiet. "You OK?" her mother asked.

7

"You know I'm going to find out sometime. I have a right to know. It should be you who tells me."

"I'm sorry, Jamie," her mother replied. "I can't."

"OK, Mom," Jamie said. "I need to go."

"Jamie? You OK?"

"I'm fine, Mom," Jamie replied. "But I've got to go now. I'll talk to you Sunday."

"Alright," her mother began, "I've got..."

Jamie hung up the phone before her mother could finish her last sentence. She did not mean to be rude, but her frustration was showing. What was it about her father that was so terrible that she was not even allowed to know his name?

She held her cell phone in her hand as she rested her arm on the sofa armrest. She blew out a deep, long breath as she turned to face out the front window again. She remained deep in thought for several moments until she opened her cell phone again and brought up the Google Maps.

Chapter 2

Jamie parked her Toyota in front of the church on the gravel shoulder of the street. It had taken her one hour and forty-three minutes to drive here. Her GPS led her directly to the front door and had predicted the arrival time nearly to the second.

The church was at the edge of town. She looked at it from the front seat of her car. She compared it to the pencil drawing from the letter Brett St. James had sent her. Other than the cemetery and the cross on the hill behind it, it looked exactly as it had been drawn. Even the stained-glass windows, that reflected brightly colored scenes from Bible stories, had been drawn in the most minute detail. The grass surrounding the church and the hillside was a deep, rich green. The longer grass on the hillside moved in waves as the wind blew across it.

She looked to see if there was a sign anywhere that would identify the name of the church or perhaps what type of church it was. There was nothing that she could see. She

guessed that it could have been a Baptist church, perhaps
Methodist, but there was no way to know.

The church had no formal parking lot. The wide gravel
shoulder of the road blended into the front lawn grass.
Jamie concluded that it served as the parking spaces. A
sidewalk extended from the shoulder of the road to the
church steps. On the other side of the street was a large field
that appeared to have once been farmland but was now
overgrown with wild grasses and brush.

She left her car and walked the several paces to the front
steps. She paused to look around. She had expected to see
some indication as to what type of church this was, but there
was nothing. She took the steps to the stoop and
approached the door.

Jamie tried the door handle. The door was unlocked.
Although it was solid and heavy, it opened easily and
noiselessly. She stepped inside. The door began to close
behind her, so she held her hand against it and let it close
quietly.

Looking through the small vestibule she saw a man kneeling
in front of an altar on a kneeling bench. The altar was a few
inches ahead of the low stage. It was carved beautifully
with a depiction of the last supper, angels, and cherubs. It
was bordered at the top with carvings of famous scenes
from the Bible: Samson bringing down pillars; David
playing a harp; David killing a lion; Noah's ark with dozens
of animals; and Abraham about to sacrifice his son on an
altar made of stones. The man's head was bowed, and his
arms stretched out wide toward the ends of the altar.

The Legacy

Jamie stepped through the vestibule and stood at the sanctuary entrance. The sanctuary was extremely ornate. Wood carvings adorned all the walls. Each carving was light colored and polished until it shimmered in the dim light. Every corner of the sanctuary had either a finely crafted carving or a beautiful oil painting with bright colors showing scenes of nature and stories from the Bible. Each end of the blonde-wood pews was covered with their own unique carving of doves, trees, lions, angels or crosses. On the stage a few feet behind the large podium there were five large straight-backed chairs. The back of the center chair was higher than the others by at least a third. It reminded Jamie of a throne. All of them were ornately carved. The podium standing in the center of the stage at its very edge was perhaps the most beautifully carved of all. Angels blew trumpets from its top two corners, grape vines wrapped around it, and at its center was an empty cross with the sun shining behind it. An empty tomb was carved along the right side of its front edge. Three women tentatively approached the tomb from the left side.

Jamie had seen churches she considered beautiful before, but she had never seen one like this. It had to be one of the most beautiful churches in the state, comparable to anything anywhere in the country. It was amazing that such a church was found in some small town that no one had ever heard of called, Amison.

She watched the man as he knelt before the altar. She heard his murmuring prayer, but the words were too soft for her to make out. After a moment he raised his head slowly, brought his hands together in front of him and stood. He rose to his full height, tall and thin, then bowed his head again. He was wearing bib overalls with a long-sleeved shirt. He stood perfectly still and quiet. Jamie waited a moment and then cleared her throat to attract his attention.

The man startled and turned quickly to look at her, wild eyed. He squatted down as if he were deciding which way to run. He turned his head from side to side, appearing to look for the nearest escape route. Jamie saw his face for the first time. He appeared to be around sixty years old. His face was clean shaven, and his full head of white hair was neatly combed.

"I'm sorry," Jamie said. "I didn't mean to startle you."

The man remained poised to run and stared at her. His eyes bulged in terror.

Jamie took one step forward. The man stepped back until he bumped up against the altar.

"I'm sorry to bother you," Jamie said. "But I'm looking for Brett St. James. Can I find him here?"

The man visibly relaxed and stood to his full height. He cocked his head to one side and looked at her. His frightened eyes narrowed with curiosity. His stare was uncomfortable.

"Is Brett St. James here?" Jamie prompted again.

The man cocked his head in the other direction. "Jamie?" he asked in a soft voice. He took a step forward and asked again, "Jamie?"

"Yes," Jamie replied. "That's me." The man walked slowly towards her. "Are you Brett St. James?" Jamie asked.

"Brett," the man said calmly as he touched his chest. He pointed a finger at Jamie. "Jamie."

Jamie held out the letter and unfolded it to let him see the note as he walked slowly toward her. "Did you send me this?" she asked.

He began stooping down the closer he came to her. He cocked his head more to the side and stepped closer to her leading with his shoulder. He pointed again at her. "Jamie, yes, Jamie," he said. "Real?"

Jamie was becoming very uncomfortable. "What?" she asked. The man was not acting normal. How did he know her? Certainly, she had never seen him before. She was beginning to think she had made a mistake in coming here. She had not told anyone where she was going. Now a fear was taking hold in her that if something were to happen, no one would know where she was. She took a half step backwards towards the door.

"Jamie," he said again as he stopped just outside of arm's reach. He was much taller than she was. He stooped down to her level and searched her eyes. "Real?" he asked again.

Jamie was frozen in place. She tried to speak but her voice caught. She cleared her throat and said, "I'm Jamie Fulton. Did you, did you send me this letter?" She held it up again for him to see. He did not look at it but kept his eyes focused intensely on her.

He unexpectedly jumped forward and touched her on the shoulder with his finger. Jamie let out a startled cry, and the man quickly shuffled backwards, out of reach again. He paused and furrowed his eyebrows. He stood to his full height and turned from her. "No, no," he said as he put both palms against his temples and stepped back towards the altar. "No, no, no, Jamie. You should not be here. You should not be here." He walked rapidly towards the altar and stopped in front of it. "I promised," he said. "Stupid, stupid, stupid, so stupid." He used his palms to hit both sides of his head each time he said the word stupid. "I promised."

He turned quickly and faced her again with a furrowed brow. "Why are you here? I promised. Why are you here?" he asked so quickly that his words nearly blended together.

"You sent me this letter," Jamie said. Her own worried look reflected his.

"No," he said. "No! No! No!" He turned and faced the altar and began hitting his palms against his temples again. "Stupid, stupid, stupid. So stupid. Noooo. Why? Why? I promised. Stupid, stupid, stupid."

"Are you OK?" Jamie spoke loudly towards his back. She took another half step backward toward the doors.

"So stupid," the man said again, as he shook his head wildly from side to side. He froze in place for a moment then turned quickly to face her and snapped to a stiff, straight posture. He shot his right arm straight up with a finger pointing skyward. "Jamie," he said loudly as his face brightened, "pray, pray twice a day and then pray thrice on Sunday!"

The change was abrupt and startling. Jamie took a full step back. He held that posture, facing upward. "Pray, pray twice a day and then pray thrice on Sunday," he repeated with a wide smile. His pose was triumphant.

The church doors opened behind her. An older woman stepped in quickly followed by a large muscular man in jeans and a grease-smeared, white T-shirt. Jamie turned to step aside, to let them step by her, but the woman stopped and stood directly in front of her. The man maneuvered himself between Jamie and the sanctuary. He squinted angrily at her. The woman reminded Jamie of a stern school teacher. She panted deeply to catch her breath.

"Who are you?" the woman asked harshly as she pointed at Jamie's chest. "What are you doing here? Are you a reporter?" The woman was her height and stood close enough that Jamie could feel her breath blowing against her face with each word. "Are you with the state?"

Jamie arched back and held up the letter between her and the woman. The woman leaned back to read it. "Mr. St. James sent me this letter," Jamie told her. "I didn't mean to upset anyone."

The woman read the letter quickly. "Who's your father?" she asked harshly.

"I, I don't know," Jamie stammered back.

The woman looked at Jamie with a scowl as if appraising Jamie's veracity. She leaned in towards her. Jamie twisted to her right and stepped backwards quickly towards the church doors. "You don't need to be coming here," the woman said angrily after her.

"I'm sorry," Jamie said as she pushed open the door. She turned to look over her shoulder for one more look at the man she came to see. He was gone.

Chapter 3

Jamie poured a cup of tea. After four hours of lying in bed and trying to get to sleep, she had given up and decided to watch a little early morning TV. She hoped that would take her mind off what happened in Amison and help her to relax. The encounter with Brett St. James and the woman that chased her away had unnerved her. The man was obviously not right, but he knew her name. That was frightening. Some man she did not know, someone with obvious mental issues, knew her name and knew her well enough to send a letter to her home address. He knew where she lived. How could someone from a little town she had never heard of, on the far side of Columbus, know so much about her? Any answer that came to mind frightened her. Perhaps it was time to get a dog.

As if the cat had read her mind, it followed her into the living room and stretched its back. "Hi, Sheba," Jamie said to it. "Come to see what's going on?" The cat walked casually to her feet and then lightly jumped into her lap. It lay down and immediately began a soft purring. "That's my girl," Jamie said, as she lightly stroked its head.

17

Jamie's mind skipped from thought to thought. Did Brett St. James, if that was him, really know anything about her father? If he did, what did he know? If he knew anything at all, could he tell her in a way that made sense? The woman that had seemed so threatening, that had chased her out of the church, had asked if she was a reporter. Why would she ask that?

"You shouldn't be here," he had said. Why not? Why shouldn't she be there? Was it because she was not allowed to be there or because it was too dangerous for her to be there? What did he mean? In her mind's eye she saw him repeatedly hitting his temples with the palms of his hands while saying, "Stupid, stupid, stupid." What was that all about? He said he had promised. Promised what? Promised who?

Was that man really Brett St. James? She could not imagine that the man she met in the church was capable of writing a letter to her or drawing such a beautiful picture. None of the things she had seen or experienced seemed to make any sense when viewed together. Was he insane? Was he an artist? Was he Brett St. James? Could he be all three?

The cat turned its head and licked her hand once. Sheba turned on its back and opened itself up for Jamie to stroke its belly. Jamie smiled and scratched the cat lightly with the tips of her fingers as it wrapped its paws around her hand.

A thought occurred to her. She wondered if the man had a guardian. Someone with such obvious issues would need someone to watch over and take care of him. Did he have family in town? Her mind raced. If he had a guardian, then that person would be someone she could talk to, someone to

18

ask about the letter, someone perhaps, that could answer questions about her father. She relaxed as a new plan began to form. The cat nipped at her hand, scrambled to its feet and jumped back to the floor.

~~~~

After attending the early church service, Jamie and her mother caught up with each other in the vestibule. Their normal Sunday routine included dinner at her mother's house. "Sorry, Mom," Jamie told her. "I've got someplace that I have to be this afternoon."

"Where are you going?" her mother asked.

"Just for a drive somewhere," she answered.

Her mother cast her eyes down for a moment and then looked back up at her. "Are you still mad at me?"

Jamie was genuinely puzzled. "Mad about what?"

"Mad about that whole father thing."

Jamie shook her head. "No, Mom. I'm not mad at you. I know someday when you're ready you'll tell me."

"Well, thank you, Jamie," her mother said. "I feel bad about the whole thing and I really wouldn't want you mad at me over it."

"I'm not mad, Mom."

"Good," her mother said smiling. "Are you sure you can't come for dinner?"

"No, sorry," Jamie answered. "I really do have someone I need to meet up with."

"Alright, but call me tonight, OK?"

"I will."

~~~~

The drive to Amison was uneventful. The Sunday traffic was light as she skirted Columbus. She drove slowly through town and parked in the gravel parking lot of the Amison Café alongside a rusting Ford pickup truck. The gravel crunched loudly as she parked in line with a handful of other cars in the lot. Since it was just after the noon hour, she assumed the restaurant would have a small crowd inside.

As she stepped inside, she was greeted by a pleasant woman who led her to a booth and handed her a menu. Jamie looked around the room. There were perhaps a dozen tables and an equal number of booths. For a small-town restaurant, it was nicer than she had expected. The floor appeared to be new linoleum. Even the legs of the tables and booths seemed newer, their chrome legs glimmering with the sunlight pouring in through the windows. The artwork on the walls included pictures of people posing with whom she assumed would be local celebrities, shaking hands, with their arms around each other, all of them smiling brightly.

The Legacy

A smiling waitress approached her with a glass of water and introduced herself as Shelly. Shelly asked if she needed a few more minutes to look over the menu and Jamie confirmed that she did.

Jamie observed the other patrons. There were a couple of families with small children, a family with two older teenaged daughters and a handful of older couples. In the far corner, four men crowded into a booth and talked together over their coffee. Everyone appeared to be dressed as if they had just come from church. The women were dressed nicely in either dresses or slacks and several men wore suits or dress pants with button-down collar shirts.

She watched as the waitress brought out plates of food to one family with children. The two boys appeared to be twins, ten or eleven years old and their daughter was seven or eight. When the waitress left the table, the family held hands, bowed their heads and said grace. Jamie smiled at the sight of the family praying. She ate out frequently, but rarely did she see anyone praying before their meals in a restaurant.

Jamie reviewed the menu, settled on a salad and set her menu on the edge of the table. Shelly immediately approached her booth.

"Ready to order?" Shelly asked.

"Yes," Jamie replied. "I'll have the house salad with a vinaigrette dressing and a cup of coffee please."

Shelly nodded without taking notes. "Sure," Shelly responded with a smile. "Anything else?"

"That's it," Jamie replied with a smile. "Thank you."

"My pleasure," Shelly said as she picked the menu up off the table. "I'll be right back with your coffee."

Shelly turned and walked towards the kitchen. She returned only a moment later with a coffee pot, cup and saucer. She placed the cup on the table and filled it. She set a handful of small cups of packaged creamer next to the cup. "I'll be back in a couple of minutes with your salad," she told Jamie smiling. She turned and walked away quickly.

Jamie pulled out her cell phone, checked her emails and scrolled through her Facebook timeline. She opened the Google Maps app again, switched it to satellite view and examined Amison from pictures taken high above it. The town was small. It was centered on the intersection of a two-lane highway and a gravel road. The intersection had the only blinker light in town.

The main street through Amison appeared to be the only fully paved road for several miles in any direction. Most of the roads anywhere around Amison were gravel. A higher view of the satellite photos showed farm after farm lined up next to each other in large square patches. The hill behind the church was the only hill in any direction. It was surrounded by farms on two sides, the church and town. It was an anomaly in a flat, featureless county.

Shelly returned with her salad and placed it on the table in front of her. "There you are," she said. "Would you like anything else?"

"No, thank you," Jamie replied with a smile as she picked up her fork.

The waitress turned but Jamie stopped her before she could step away. "Oh, Shelly?" Jamie asked. Shelly turned back around and faced the table again with a smile. "I have a question that maybe you can help me with," Jamie told her.

"Sure," Shelly replied happily.

"That church down at the end of the street," Jamie said as she pointed in the direction of the church. "What kind of church is that?"

"It used to be a Methodist church," Shelly answered. "It's not really a church anymore."

"Then what is it now? It looks like it's being used as a church."

"No," Shelly replied. "Someone lives there now."

Jamie cocked her head. "We can't be talking about the same church. I mean the one that's about two blocks that way," she said as she pointed in the direction of the church again. "That one down there that has the bell tower and the cemetery by it. It's really pretty inside with lots of wood carvings."

The smile dropped from Shelly's face and she stared blankly at Jamie for a moment. Shelly's warm smile suddenly seemed cool and her face took on added color. "You've been inside?" Shelly asked in a quiet tone.

"Yes," Jamie answered. "Just inside the sanctuary."

Shelly was slow to respond. "Why?" she asked as her eyes squinted.

The waitress suddenly appeared very uncomfortable. Jamie tried to choose her words carefully. "I was looking for a man by the name of Brett St. James. He sent me this letter." She pulled the envelope with the letter from her purse and held it up for Shelly to see. Jamie removed the two pages, unfolded them on the table and turned both pages towards Shelly.

Shelly looked down at the letter and narrowed her eyes at it. She read the brief note and looked over the picture. After a moment she looked up at Jamie. "I'm sorry," she said as she tried to force a smile. "I really can't help you."

She turned and took a step before Jamie could try to stop her. "I'm trying to find his guardian," she said, raising her voice slightly. Shelly hesitated, then continued toward the kitchen.

Jamie watched as the woman pushed through the kitchen door. Why had the waitress responded that way? What nerve had she struck? Why had she seemed surprised, almost angry that she had been inside? If it was not a church, then what was it? It certainly did not look as if someone lived there.

She ate her salad and looked around the restaurant to see if there was anyone else, she may be able to approach. The waitress returned, topped off her coffee cup and left without a smile or an acknowledgment when Jamie thanked her. Jamie had nearly finished her coffee when a man approached her table. Jamie looked up from her cell phone, as he approached.

"Hi," he said, as he began to seat himself across the booth from her, uninvited. "Can I join you for a moment?" Jamie was startled at his assertiveness and took a short breath in. She recognized the man as being one of the four men that were sitting together in the booth at the other end of the restaurant. He was an older man with thick gray hair. He wore a shirt and tie and smiled warmly at her. She glanced at the remaining three men. They were watching.

He reached over the table towards her, offering to shake her hand. "I'm Pete, but people around here call me Doc."

"Jamie," she answered as she shook his hand.

"Are you with the state?" Doc asked.

"No," Jamie responded.

"Are you a reporter?"

"No," she replied as she gave him a puzzled look.

"Why are you asking about the church?"

Jamie paused for a deep breath. "I'm looking for someone. Someone sent me a letter and asked me to meet them at the church."

"Who sent you the letter?" Doc asked.

Jamie pulled the letter out again from her purse and spread the pages open on the table and turned it toward Doc. "Brett St. James," Jamie said.

Doc glanced briefly at the drawing, then gently lifted the first page from the table and read it silently. "Who's your father?" he asked her as he looked up.

"I don't know," Jamie replied. "That's kind of why I'm here. I'm trying to see if I can find any information about him."

Doc tilted his head up and looked at her. He seemed to consider what she had told him, pursed his lips and nodded. "I don't think you'll find out anything here," he said as he returned the paper to the table. "Have you met Mr. St. James?"

Jamie nodded. "Yes, if that was him in the church."

"Then I think, as you've probably seen, Mr. St. James can't hold a conversation, especially with strangers."

"Could you tell me who his guardian is?" Jamie asked him.

Doc sucked his cheeks in, pursed his lips and shook his head. "His guardian? No, I'm sorry," he told her. "I would think that technically, his guardian would be his son. He comes around every couple of weeks to check on him, but Brett takes care of himself."

"He takes care of himself?" Jamie questioned.

Doc shrugged his shoulders and opened the palms of his hands upwards and towards her. "Yeah," he said, "he does.

26

The people around here help him out when he needs something, but he's doing OK."

Jamie stared into the man's eyes looking for any hint of deception. "He knew my name," she told him. "When he saw me, he said my name. He knew who I was." Doc opened his mouth to say something, but Jamie continued before he began. "And how would he know my home address? He sent me this letter." She tapped the opened letter laying on the table with her finger. "How would he know where I live?"

Doc shrugged again. "I dunno," he answered. "I can't explain that. Maybe you two met before and you just don't remember." He pointed toward the letter's envelope. "May I see that?" he asked.

Jamie slid the envelope across the table to him. He held it up to let the light shine through it. Seeing nothing worth noting, he checked the postmark. "It's postmarked from Columbus," he said. "That's normal for around here since we don't have a post office." He handed the envelope back to her. "Like I said, you probably met him before and you just don't remember."

"No," Jamie said confidently. "I've never seen him before in my life and I've got to tell you that I'm a little freaked about it. He sends me this letter and offers to tell me something about my father. When I come here to meet him, he acted…" Jamie paused, trying to choose her words carefully, "strange. And then two people, who I assumed *might* have been his guardians, run me off."

Doc nodded his understanding. "I think I can explain the two people that ran you off. That was probably Ben and his mother, Ruth. They both work just down the street from the church in the garage. When they see cars parked out front of the church, they check it out. There's a lot of valuable artwork in there and they'd like to protect it, we'd all like to protect it." He paused for a moment, then added, "and Brett."

"So, that *was* Brett St. James," Jamie said without emotion. Doc nodded. "Why did she ask if I was a reporter?" Jamie asked.

"You saw the building," he told her. "Every once in a while, someone comes around and wants to do a story on the church. We're really not interested in having anyone printing pictures of our little church in any magazine or paper. It would bring too many people around. We like it quiet and so does Brett."

Jamie relaxed. She exhaled as she slumped imperceptivity in her seat and took another deep breath. She let it out slowly through pursed lips. "I'd like to know how he knows me," she told Doc.

Doc shrugged again. "I don't know how to help you. You really can't ask him. He couldn't tell you." Doc paused for a moment, then said, "I'll talk to his son when he comes around next Saturday. If he knows anything, I'll have him call you if that's OK."

"OK," Jamie told him. "If that's the best we can do."

"Can I make a copy of the letter to show him? He'd be interested."

"That's fine," she replied.

Doc signaled to Shelly, who was watching from the nearby kitchen. Shelly approached the table and faced Doc with her back to Jamie. "Do you have something that can copy this?" Doc asked her, as he held the two papers up towards her.

"I think I can," Shelly answered. "Ken's got a copier in his office. I'll see what I can do."

She took the paper from Doc and walked away briskly. It occurred to Jamie that now that the letter had left her possession, she might not be able to get it back. She pushed the thought aside.

"Why is she mad at me?" she asked Doc.

"Why would you think she's mad at you?" he asked her.

"She just looks like I offended her or something."

"Nah," Doc answered. "The people around here are a little protective about Brett and the church. They worry when people they don't know suddenly show up asking about either him or the church. They think that someone might try to take him away. She probably thinks you're a social worker or something. She'll be fine."

They sat in silence for a moment before Jamie spoke. "What's the story with the church?"

"No story, really," he said. "Several years back it just sat empty. Brett bought it. I guess he just liked the place."

"That man bought that place?" Jamie asked with a sense of surprise. "How's that possible?"

Doc used his hands to make a shrugging motion on the table. "He wasn't always like this. At one time he was as normal as you and I are."

"So, what happened to him?" She asked. "Alzheimer's?"

"I dunno," he answered as he shrugged. "Maybe. Might be something else. I'm not his doctor."

"What?" Jamie asked.

Shelly returned to the table with the letter and a copy of it. She handed the copy to Doc, then dropped the letter on the table in front of Jamie.

"Thanks, Shell," Doc said as he folded the paper in thirds.

Doc returned his attention to Jamie. "I think I've told you all I can about Mr. St. James," he said. "But I'll tell you this: The whole town likes him and will do anything to protect him. It's probably not a good idea to come around and bother him."

Jamie's face flushed with the implied threat. She looked Doc directly in the eyes and held his stare. A moment passed before she looked away. "Alright," she told him. "But if he sends me another letter, then you know I'll have to be back. I'll have to know."

"I understand," Doc replied as he nodded. "I'm sorry I interrupted your lunch. I'll let you get back at it." He began to slide out of the booth but stopped. "Oh, I'll need your number to give to Brett's son."

"Sure," Jamie replied as she reached into her purse for a pen. Doc handed her his folded copy of the letter. She wrote her cell phone number on the back of it.

Doc took the pen and wrote his own number on a napkin. "If you have any questions, please call me. I'll be glad to answer anything I can." Jamie nodded at him. He left the booth and returned to rejoin his three friends.

Jamie looked down at her half-eaten salad and took a sip of her coffee. It was beginning to get cold, so she drank the cup empty and began picking at her salad again. She had expected that Shelly would come around and refill her cup but that was not going to happen.

Before Jamie had finished the last of her meal, Shelly returned with a handwritten bill. "Thanks for coming in," she said without a smile. She turned, walked back towards the kitchen and ducked out of view. Jamie saw Doc looking at her. He gave her a smile and a nod and turned back to his conversation with the other men.

Jamie took the slip of paper to the cash register at the front entrance. She was met there by an older woman who took the bill from her. Jamie handed her a twenty-dollar bill. As she waited for her change, she noticed a wood carving on the window ledge behind the woman. It was a carving of two dolphins jumping out of the water.

The woman gave her the change without saying anything. Jamie tucked the change in her wallet but kept out a five-dollar bill. She saw Shelly staring at her from the kitchen door with a stern face. Jamie tilted her head and smiled. She returned to her booth and placed the five-dollar bill gently on the table as she turned her head towards Shelly.

Shelly sneered and ducked out of view. Jamie glanced back at Doc who was looking at her again. He waved his hand and smiled kindly. Jamie reflexively waved back before turning and leaving the restaurant.

She had climbed in her car and put the key in the ignition when she saw Brett St. James walking on the sidewalk that ran alongside the gravel parking lot. His shoulders were hunched, and his head hung low. Walking slowly, he looked down at the concrete, shaking his head and moving his mouth as if he were having a loud argument with himself. He carried several plastic grocery bags. Through the thin plastic, Jamie could see that they were packed with grocery items. She assumed that he was returning from shopping at the small store up the street.

Jamie opened the door and stood behind it with her hands gripping the top of the car door window. He was only a few feet in front of her when she called out to him. "Mr. St. James?" she asked loudly. St. James made no indication that he heard her. "Brett?" she prompted again.

Without raising his head, St. James stopped and turned towards her. He looked at her a moment. "Not real," he mumbled and continued walking towards the church.

Jamie closed the car door and jogged to catch up with him. She walked shoulder to shoulder with him. There was no indication that he realized she was with him. He began quietly repeating in a sing-song manner, "Pray, pray twice a day, and then pray thrice on Sunday".

"Mr. St. James?" Jamie prompted.

St. James stopped and turned to face her. He looked confused. "No," he said. "Rene will be mad." He bowed his head and began walking again as he chanted, "Pray, pray twice a day and then pray thrice on Sunday."

"It's me," Jamie said. "Jamie Fulton."

St. James stopped again and looked at her. He shook his head. "No," he said more forcefully. "Rene doesn't know." He turned and began walking again. "No, no, no, no," he repeated, shaking his head wildly. "Not real," he said more quietly. "Not real. Pray, pray twice a day and then pray thrice on Sunday."

Doc hurried towards her from the restaurant entrance followed by two other men and a woman. Doc put his arm around Jamie's shoulder and smiled pleasantly towards her as he directed her back towards the parking lot. The woman moved quickly to Brett's side. He was several inches taller than her and she had to reach up to put her hand on his shoulder. She looked up at him and spoke so softly to Brett that Jamie could not hear what she was saying. One of the other men stood off the edge of the sidewalk, keeping his eyes fixed on Jamie and Doc as they passed by in front of him. Doc directed her back to her car. The third man walked two paces behind the woman and St. James.

Doc spoke to Jamie condescendingly. "Let's not bother Mr. St. James, shall we?"

They walked slowly together towards Jamie's car in the parking lot. Jamie glanced over her shoulder to see the woman walking slowly with St. James with her hand on his shoulder. "I only wanted to find out how he knew me," Jamie told Doc. "Or what he knows about my father."

"Well, Jamie," Doc said. "I'm sorry. But I don't think Mr. St. James could tell you even if he remembered. Why not let's just leave it alone, OK?"

Jamie brushed off Doc's arm from around her shoulder and continued walking toward her car. She looked up into his face as she walked. "What is it with you people? All I'd like to do is ask him a question."

"I understand," Doc answered. "I really do. But like I said before, we're pretty protective of our friends around here and there isn't anything that he'll be able to tell you. Just talking to a stranger could cause problems."

They walked shoulder to shoulder back to Jamie's car. Doc opened the door for her and Jamie climbed in. Doc held the door open a moment longer than necessary. "Jamie," he said, "please let this go. There really isn't anything here for you."

Jamie reached for the door handle to close the door behind her. Doc closed it gently for her and stepped back. She put the car in reverse, pulled out and headed home.

Chapter 4

It had been almost three weeks since the encounter at the restaurant. On the way home from work, Jamie stopped to check her mailbox at the subdivision entrance. As soon as she opened the mailbox door, the strong scent of a man's cologne wafted up towards her. The beige business sized letter was the only item inside the box. It was addressed to her in the same block lettered handwriting that was on the first letter she received from Brett St. James. She held the letter to her nose and sniffed. It was a pleasant fragrance, but she furrowed her eyebrows with the returning tension.

Seated back in her car, she opened the letter by tearing off an end of the envelope. There was no written note this time. The single page was filled corner to corner with a drawing, shaded with water color. The picture was of her. She stared at it gape mouthed. The picture was of her standing inside of the Amison church sanctuary. The drawing was complete in every detail as she remembered it, from the ornate carvings on the pews to the wall art. It showed her exactly as she was dressed the day she stood in that very position at the church. It was as if the picture had been drawn from a photograph. Her expression appeared worried, or perhaps frightened. Jamie was certain that the picture was from the perspective that Brett St. James had at the exact moment he first laid his startled eyes on her.

Since her encounter in the Amison restaurant, she had nearly put the entire episode behind her and out of her mind. The letter brought it all to the forefront of her attention again. The encounter was intimidating. Doc had seemed threatening even though he smiled and spoke softly. There was nothing specific that she could point to, but he clearly intended to be intimidating and he succeeded. Now, with this new drawing in hand, her heart raced. It made her want to go back to Amison one more time. She wanted to meet with Brett St. James again, but she did not expect that she would have any more luck than the first two times.

Returning home, Jamie put the opened letter on the kitchen island and changed out of her work clothes. She took a cold bottle of soda from the refrigerator and sat down on a barstool at the island. Sheba brushed against Jamie's foot and meowed at her. "Just a second, sweetie," Jamie told her. "I'll get you some dinner in just a minute."

She held the drawing and examined it closely. It appeared as if it had been shaded in with both colored pencils and watercolor. The artwork was remarkable for its beauty. If it was not for the frightened expression on her face, she would have gladly framed it and hung it on her living room wall.

The scent of the cologne was pervasive, filling the surrounding air. She sniffed the paper and wondered about the letter. Why did he send this to her? What purpose did it serve? Did he still want to tell her something about her father? There was no note attached this time. These were questions she did not have answers to. To ask St. James about them would require her to avoid the townspeople, but she had no idea how she would do that.

She wondered if she could bring a couple of large male friends to run interference for her while she tried to talk to Brett. She considered asking Phil, her coworker. She had envisioned the woman and man she had encountered at the first meeting confronting her again. Phil would step in to defend her. She did not think that would end well for anyone. She decided against it.

The cat jumped onto the kitchen island, meowed loudly and forced itself between Jamie's arms and pushed its nose against her lips. "OK, OK, you're hungry. I get it," she said as she stroked the cat. Jamie opened a can of cat food, placed it in the cat's bowl and refilled a second bowl with water. The cat purred while it ate. "Bon appétit," Jamie told her before returning her attention to the drawing.

Jamie took the drawing and soda with her and sat down on the sofa. She held the picture with one hand and with the other, took sips of her soda. She reran the conversation with Doc through her mind. Doc had said that Brett's son came around every couple of weeks to check up on him. When she talked to Doc, Brett's son was expected that next Saturday. That was almost three weeks ago. Perhaps, if she went back to the church this weekend, she could meet up with him. A surge of energy flowed through her. She would have to find a way not to be run off by the townspeople before she had a chance to see him. Her mind wandered from possibility to possibility. She settled on a plan. She would stay outside of town but remain close enough to see if a car parked in front of the church. If one did, she would assume it was Brett's son and then she would pull up to the church to introduce herself.

~~~~

Saturday Jamie parked about a half mile away along the edge of the road. A large tree shaded her car. Her hands were shaky. Would anyone from town notice her car parked this far away? With her binoculars, she could easily see if anyone parked in front of the church, but she was far enough away that she hoped no one would recognize her car, hopefully not even notice her.

She had arrived at eight that morning. Not knowing when or if Brett's son would be coming that day meant that she could have a long wait for nothing. Would his son arrive in the morning or in the afternoon? Would he stay for an hour or would he stay all day? Since she did not know any of these answers, she would have to come early and perhaps stay late. Even then, Brett's son may not come at all, making the entire day a waste of time.

About an hour into her wait she saw a young teenager on a bicycle riding towards her on the opposite side of the road. She watched him as he approached. Was he looking at her? He was. He was looking directly at her. Several cars had passed by in both directions since she arrived. None of them had paid any attention to her, but seeing this kid coming towards her gave her butterflies in her stomach.

As he came closer, she could see he had long ginger hair that blew back behind him from under a green John Deere hat. He wore mirrored sunglasses, jeans and a red T-shirt with a logo on it she did not recognize. The bicycle squeaked with every pedal. He rode past her car on the opposite side of the

road. He kept his eyes on her as he coasted by. As Jamie
began to relax, she saw him turning around in her rearview
mirror. He rolled up beside her passenger side door,
dropped off the seat and straddled the bike's top bar. He
looked in through the window. Jamie put her hand on the
keys, ready to start the car and drive off when he spoke
loudly enough to be heard through the closed window.
"Are you Jamie?"

Jamie looked at him nervously. "Yes," she answered.

"Doc says you should come down to the church and wait.
Mr. St. James should be here any time."

Jamie stared at him blankly. She had avoided driving
through town. She had tried to park far enough away that
no one would recognize her. How did they? How did they
know what she wanted?

Jamie tried to speak, had to clear her throat and then tried
again. "Doc?" she asked weakly.

"Mr. Allison," he said. "Doc. He says you met him at the
restaurant. He says you don't have to sit out here in the
boonies. You can come into town. He says he'll bring you a
cup of coffee if you want to wait in front of the church. He
said just don't go inside until Mr. St. James gets here."

"OK," she replied nervously. "I'll be there in a few minutes.

The boy nodded at her, spun a pedal backward until it was
at its high point and pedaled off. Jamie took several deep
breaths, trying to calm herself. She watched the clock on her
radio until it incremented five minutes before she started the
car. She drove slowly into town. By the time she parked her

car in front of the church the boy had already ridden past the church and was parking his bike outside of the restaurant.

Jamie left the car running and the windows rolled up. She kept her eyes turned downtown and nervously checked her mirrors and surroundings frequently. She saw few people and any cars that passed by her were all just passing through.

Doc came out of the restaurant. He was carrying a large Styrofoam cup of what she assumed to be coffee with him. He walked towards her at a casual pace. He smiled as he approached her car.

He held the coffee in one hand and tapped the window with the other. Jamie rolled the window down a couple of inches. "I talked to David on the phone a few minutes ago," Doc told her. "He was already on his way. He should be here in a few minutes."

"Thank you," Jamie replied.

"I've brought you some coffee. Two creams, right?"

She rolled down the window far enough for Doc to hand her the coffee cup. "Thank you," she said again as she took the warm cup from him.

"If you need anything, I'll be up at the restaurant."

"OK, thanks," Jamie replied.

Doc gave a quick wave of his hand and began walking back to the restaurant. Jamie pulled off the lid of the coffee cup and sniffed it. The coffee was hot and smelled fresh. She put the cup to her lips. The warmth of the coffee touched her. It was inviting. She paused a moment before taking the first sip, snapped the lid back on and placed it in the cup holder. She did not trust Doc well enough to drink anything that he would give to her.

The church appeared empty. The morning air retained its chill, but the sun was bright and shown directly on the front of the church. The light reflected brightly off its large white wooden doors. The solitary tree on the hill behind the church seemed to glow as the sun hit its spring leaves. It was peaceful and picturesque.

Movement in her rearview mirror caught her attention. A large white SUV with a Cadillac emblem on its front pulled up behind her and parked. She watched as a tall man stepped out, stretched his back and glanced up at her. He had short, dark hair and was cleanly shaven. He had an athletic build and was dressed in a tight Polo shirt, tan pants and casual shoes. It seemed to Jamie that the man may be dressed a little too lightly for the weather which was in the mid to high fifties.

The man approached Jamie's driver's side door, stood back about three feet and leaned down far enough to see Jamie's face. "Are you Jamie?" the man asked loudly to be heard through the closed window.

Jamie rolled down the window part way. "Yes," she said. "Are you Brett's son?"

"Yes, that's me," he said. "I'm David St. James."

Jamie rolled the window up, turned off the car engine and stepped out. He offered his hand to her, and she shook it. His smile was kind.

"I understand that you would like to meet my father," David said.

"Yes," she said. "If that would be OK. He sent me two letters and said he could tell me something about *my* father."

"Two letters?" David asked. "I've seen a copy of one of them. What else did he send you?"

Jamie retrieved the second letter from her purse and handed it to him. He opened it and looked at the picture. "That's me when I came to see him the first time," she told him. David smiled, nodded and handed it back to her.

"He's quite talented, isn't he," David commented.

"Very."

He cocked his head to one side as he looked at her. "You look really familiar," he told her. "I think I may have seen you somewhere before, but I don't remember ever meeting you."

"I don't think we've met before this," Jamie told him. "You don't look familiar to me."

"Hmm," David hummed. He paused a moment, then motioned toward the church. "Let's go in, shall we?" he suggested.

The Legacy

They walked together towards the church. "I understand that your father bought this church," Jamie said as they walked casually toward the front steps.

"Yes. He bought it for my mother," he replied. "My mom grew up here in Amison. She used to attend church services here. Before she passed, she wanted to come back and visit her old church. But it was closed. There hadn't been a church service in here for several years. It was getting run down. When my mom saw it, she cried for days. My dad felt so bad for her that he bought the church and had it fixed up."

"It's beautiful," Jamie commented.

"Yes," David said, "it is. My mom got to see it just before she died. We all came together to see it. When we got here, Dad had arranged for the people here in town to have a potluck dinner back behind the church on the lawn. It was like the ones the church used to have here when my mom was growing up."

David was quiet for a moment, then spoke softly. "There were several people here that remembered her from when she was a little girl and teenager. It was like a big family reunion. I remember looking over and seeing my mom sitting in a lawn chair watching everything going on and she just looked so peaceful. It was like everything was right in the world and she didn't really have cancer."

They walked up the steps of the church. David paused at the landing and stopped to look at Jamie. "She died three weeks later. She kept that peaceful look with her right up to the end." He pointed in the direction of the cemetery along the side of the church out of view. "I don't know how Dad did it, but he arranged to have my mom buried in that old cemetery here. I think the next youngest grave before that was from the forties. There are stones dating back as far as the mid-eighteen hundreds."

David pulled on the handle of the heavy white wooden door and opened it for her. They stepped into the vestibule and David let the door close quietly behind him.

"But that's when my dad started losing it. He moved into the church. Every day he goes out and sits by her grave and talks to her," David said. He waved his arm towards the sanctuary. "All the artwork you see here, all the paintings, the carvings, the altar and those big chairs up there, my dad made all that. I'm sure he doesn't sleep most nights, he just works on these pieces of art."

David led her further inside. He chose a pew, moved in and sat down. He turned sideways in the pew and rested his arm on the back of the pew. He motioned for Jamie to join him. She sat and faced him, her hands resting in her lap.

Jamie looked at David with compassion. "What happened to your dad?"

"You mean, why is he acting that way?" David asked. "I'd like to think it's because he misses my mom so much that he just checked out. But I suspect that it's Alzheimer's. At least that's what his doctor is suggesting."

"But you let him stay here all by himself?" Jamie asked.

"I could never institutionalize him, even if it were just in my home. That would be a prison for him. He's happy now in his own little world, working on his art, talking to my mom.

The Legacy

He's got an entire town looking after him. I come in every couple of weeks to visit and catch up on any bills he may owe people here in Amison. I've got people here bringing him wood to work with and other supplies. He's close to my mom, and he's happy."

"Isn't there some medication to help him?" Jamie asked.

"The doctor tried a few things. Different medications and such, but they all made him sick. We had him in the hospital once but that almost killed him. He completely shut down. I finally pulled him out and moved him in with me. He wasn't as bad then. He kept asking me to take him to the church. I thought it was just so he could visit Mom's grave but once we finally got him here, he refused to leave. He made it clear he wanted to live here. So, I made all the arrangements and let him move in."

"And there's no zoning against moving in here?" Jamie asked him.

"Well, there's a little apartment in the back there behind the stage. I had a talk with the village council and then zoning wasn't a problem."

There was a brief lag in the conversation. "Do you have any idea how your dad knows me?" Jamie asked.

"I have no idea. That's a mystery to me. There must be some connection to him in your past."

"None that I can think of," she answered. "I had never heard of Amison prior to receiving his letter."

"Is there any chance you may have worked for him in the past?"

"Where would I have worked for your father?"

"Maybe at Tashe International," he said. "Any chance you once worked for Tashe?"

"No."

"Have you ever heard of Tashe?"

"It seems like I've seen some factory buildings with that name, but I don't know anything about them."

"It's a major international automotive supply company."

"I've never worked for a factory," Jamie said.

David pondered a moment. "I really have no idea how my father knows you. We'll ask him but please don't expect much."

"Can he remember you OK?" she asked.

"Oh, yeah. He knows who I am, but he's so deep into his own world that he can hardly talk to anyone outside of it."

"That's really too bad," Jamie told him. "I feel bad for you."

David looked down, pursed his lips and nodded slowly. "You know," he said. "There are times when he looks at you and for just the briefest of moments you know he's back. He'll be completely lucid. Then it's gone," he snapped his finger, "just like that."

The conversation lagged again. "Where's he at now?" she asked.

"He's probably downstairs in the basement working on some project. That's where he's usually at when he's not sitting in the cemetery. Shall we go see?"

"Yes, please," Jamie answered.

They stood, and David guided her towards a door in the front of the sanctuary on the left side. Narrow steps led down and then sharply to the right into the basement area. Jamie followed down behind him.

The basement area was well lit with a drop ceiling and recessed lighting. The ceiling was low enough that Jamie could have easily jumped up and touched it with little effort. She was sure David could have reached up and placed his palm flat on it without extending his arm straight. The room was packed with canvas artwork and wood carvings of every size. Tables were arranged in rows, leaving only a small gap between them for aisleways. They were covered with small carved statuettes, paintings and papers with drawings tossed haphazardly around the tables. Some paintings and drawings were lying face up, others face down, but most were scrolled up and tucked between carvings. The entire room smelled of fresh cut wood and varnish.

There was a metallic tapping sound coming from a room in the back with an opened door. The tapping paused and then a lighter, quicker ticking sound followed. "He's carving in his workshop," David said as he motioned her forward behind him.

They walked the narrow aisle towards the room. Jamie was amazed at all the carvings on the tables surrounding her. There were hundreds of them, carved out of many differing sizes of wooden blocks. She could not venture to guess the total value of these carvings, but she was confident that if any one of these were for sale, she could never afford it.

David stepped into the doorway of the room and motioned for Jamie to stop where she was, out of view. "Hi, Dad," David said.

The ticking stopped. "David, David, David," she heard his father say.

"How are you doing?" David asked him.

"David, David, David," his father repeated. "Pray, pray twice a day and then pray thrice on Sunday." Jamie heard the metallic tapping begin again.

"I know, Dad. I do. What are you carving today?"

"David, David, David." Tick, tick, tick...

David stepped out of Jamie's view to the left of the door. She heard him say, "This is beautiful. What are you going to do with this one?" The tapping stopped.

"David, David, David. Pray, pray twice a day and then pray thrice on Sunday." Tick, tick, tick.

"You going to give this to one of your friends?"

"Yep. Pray, pray." Tick, tick, tick, tick...

"It's nice. I'm sure they'll like it."

The ticking stopped. "I sing today, David."

"Did you sing today? That's great, Dad."

"Pray, pray."

"I bet it sounded awesome. You have a great voice."

"Yes. Pray, pray." Tick, tick.

"Dad, I've brought somebody who would like to meet you."
The ticking stopped. There was a long silence. "It's OK,
Dad. She thinks you know her." More silence.

Jamie stepped around the corner and through the doorway.
David's back was toward her. A block of wood, about a foot
tall and half as wide was clamped to a large, heavy wooden
work table. Brett held a chisel against it with one hand and
a hammer in the other. He looked up at her and his eyes
widened. David turned his head and saw that she was
standing in the doorway.

"Dad," David began, "I'd like you to meet..."

Brett crouched down a couple of inches, hunched his body
and interrupted David with a loud whispered voice.
"David..." he said.

"Yeah, Dad?"

"I see Jamie."

"Yes, Dad. That's Jamie."

"Real?"

"Yes, Dad. She's real."

Brett slowly stood tall. He was a little taller than David when he straightened. Brett spoke in an awed voice, "Pray, pray twice a day and then pray thrice on Sunday." He reached towards her, moved forward in a slow sidestep past David. He stopped within arm's reach of Jamie. "David?" Brett asked without looking back.

"Yes, Dad?"

"Real?"

"Jamie is real, Dad."

Brett kept his eyes focused on Jamie's arm as he reached out slowly to touch her. He cautiously touched her arm below her shoulder and jerked his arm back against his chest as if he had been shocked. He looked up at Jamie's face in wide eyed amazement. "Jamie," he said in a loud whisper. "You came."

"Hi, Brett," Jamie said softly to him with a gentle smile. "I'm pleased to meet you."

Brett turned to David, "OK?"

"Yeah, Dad. It's OK."

Brett faced Jamie again. His face lit up. "Oh… Jamie," he said brightly. He spun quickly and faced David. "Jamie!" he said loudly as he pointed a finger at her.

David smiled at him. "Yes, Dad. That's Jamie."

Brett spun quickly to face her. "Oh… Jamie," he said almost reverently. "You came. You see me now."

"Yes. I'm here," Jamie said.

"Pray, pray twice a day and then pray thrice on Sunday," he said in a reverent voice. He reached out and touched her arm again, and again jerked his hand back as if he was shocked. "Jamie," he whispered softly, "but I promised." He crouched down slightly. His eyes darted wildly around the workshop. He pointed at her and said excitedly, "Oh, Jamie. Something for you."

Jamie looked at David, who gave her a small shrug.

Brett quickly slid past her through the door into the room with all the art and carvings. "Come," he said as he motioned her to follow him. He then repeated the same little song Jamie had heard before, "Pray, pray twice a day and then pray thrice on Sunday." He moved quickly with a little dance in his step to a table midway up the room. He slid between two of the tables. The passage was so narrow that he had to walk sideways between them. He bumped the wooden carvings on either side of him, jostling them around the tables. Brett ignored them all and stopped before he reached the end of the last table in the row. He reached down and picked up one of the carvings as carefully as if he were picking up a newborn baby. "Jamie," he said reverently, this time to the carving.

David and Jamie walked up the aisle until they stood at the end of the rows of tables Brett was in. "Jamie," he repeated with reverence as he stepped cautiously sideways to exit the narrow aisle. He held the carving in front of him by the fingertips of both hands. When he emerged from between the two rows of tables, he turned and faced Jamie. He hunched over and held the carving out to her as he looked in her eyes over the top of it. "Jamie," he said softly.

"For me?" Jamie asked as she reached for the carving.

"Jamie," Brett said again.

Jamie took the carving from him and then turned it to see its front. The carving was made from a light, blonde, unvarnished block of wood. It was a carving of a girl angel standing on a cloud. It had angel wings folded behind it that rose above her head. She had a long robe on and was holding a small scroll tied with a ribbon in one hand and a large thin book in the other. Her hair cascaded out from under a graduation cap and a fragile, finely carved tassel hung from the left side of the cap.

Jamie gasped and looked up at Brett, who squealed in delight. "Jamie, Jamie, Jamie!" he said excitedly. He moved quickly back between the tables, carelessly knocking carvings off the tables and onto the floor. "Jamie, Jamie, Jamie!" he repeated rapidly.

Jamie held the carving at eye level and turned to look at David.

"What's wrong?" David asked her.

"It's me," she said. "I'm the angel." She turned the carving to face David so that he could see it. The face of the angel was clearly Jamie.

David's mouth dropped open as he looked back up at Jamie, speechless.

"That's me when I graduated OU," she said. "He gave me angel wings."

"Jamie, Jamie, Jamie," Brett said in a singsong voice. "Pray, pray twice a day." He came quickly back to Jamie holding another carving and held it out excitedly to Jamie.

Jamie handed the first carving to David and took the second carving from Brett carefully. It was a carving of a young girl singing while holding a music folder in front of her. "That's me, too," she said. "That's me when I was just a girl. I must have been singing in church or in school."

Brett stepped back-and-forth sideways from foot to foot in an excited dance.

"Brett," Jamie said. "It's beautiful. It's me."

"Jamie, Jamie, Jamie!"

He danced up the isle from table to table pointing in the general directions of many carvings. "Jamie, Jamie, Jamie. Jamie, Jamie, Jamie." When he reached the end of the room, he turned to face them, stretched his arms outward and up, lifted his head and said loudly, "Jamie, Jamie, Jamie!" He was breathless, nearly panting. His face beamed.

Jamie began looking at the carvings on the table. There were carvings of many types, angels, animals, dolphins, men and boys, but whenever an angel, a girl or a woman was carved, it was always with her face, the face of Jamie.

She stopped and looked at Brett, who was standing at the end of the aisle. His hands were clasped in front of him. He looked like a child who was worried that a parent would not like his art project. "Brett," she said. "They're beautiful!"

Brett instantly grinned broadly, squealed and spun around as he held his arms out, side-to-side. He spun around several times. "Jamie, Jamie, Jamie," he repeated.

He stopped spinning and looked at Jamie. His face glowed with delight. Jamie looked at him and returned his smile. "They're beautiful, Brett," she said again. "Thank you. Thank you." Brett clasped his hands in front of his chest and smiled at her shyly.

Jamie turned to look at David who was standing several feet behind her. He was stunned. She turned and looked again at Brett who now appeared embarrassed. "They're all so beautiful, Brett," she told him. "But why me? How do you know me?"

Brett looked down at the floor. "Jamie, Jamie, Jamie," he said softly.

"Brett," she said, "how do you know me?"

Brett did not look up. "Pray, pray twice a day. How do I know Jaymay?" He asked quietly, rhyming her name with 'pray.' He hung his head lower and Jamie saw a tear falling silently to the floor.

"Oh, Brett," Jamie said with compassion as she took a step forward. Brett looked up at her, gasped and took a step back. He suddenly appeared to be afraid.

Jamie stopped, frozen in place a few feet from him. She saw the panic rising in him. "Brett," she said. "Can I give you a hug?"

Brett looked at her with worried eyes. Tears had streaked his cheeks through a fine layer of sawdust. Jamie remained where she was, motionless, afraid that she was frightening him. Slowly, as if fighting through his fear, he raised his arms out towards her. Jamie's smile broadened, and she moved cautiously towards him, stopping again within arm's reach. The worried, frightened look remained on his face and another tear rolled down from his left eye. Jamie slowly moved in the rest of the way and put her arms around him and squeezed him tightly with her ear pressed against his chest. Cautiously, Brett wrapped his arms gently around her and rubbed his hand up and down her back. "Jamie," he whispered.

~~~~

Jamie and David sat facing each other in the front pew. Brett sat on the edge of the pew directly behind them, sitting tall with his back straight. His hands gripped the back of the pew between them.

David had wiped Brett's face and cleaned the tear-streaked sawdust away. Now Brett smiled at them broadly with his lips pressed tightly together. Every several seconds Brett would reach up and softly touch Jamie with one or two fingers on her shoulder as if he still wanted to be sure she was actually there. Once he reached up and brushed the back of her hair and pulled quickly away as Jamie turned to look at him. He looked frightened, but Jamie chuckled at him and touched him back on the shoulder. Brett relaxed and said, "Jamie," with an awed reverence.

"I give up," David said. "I have no idea how he knows you."

"I don't know," she replied. She turned the carving of her as a young girl singing around in her hands. "But he's obviously known me at least since I was this age."

Brett put his hand on David's shoulder, leaned in and whispered loudly, "David?"

"Yes, Dad."

Brett whispered more quietly, "sister." He turned his head to look at Jamie and smiled at her.

David and Jamie looked at each other stunned. Brett then leaned towards Jamie and whispered loudly, "brother," as he turned to look back again at David.

There was a stunned silence as David and Jamie looked back and forth between each other and then back at Brett. Their jaws hung open. Brett leaned back and sat upright on the edge of the pew again. He turned his head back and forth, looking at the two of them. He was grinning wildly like a proud schoolboy.

David shook himself from his stunned silence first. "Dad," he said as he looked at Brett, "are you trying to say that Jamie and I are brother and sister?"

"Yes!" Brett shouted as he shot both arms straight upward as if his favorite football team had just scored. He tilted his head towards the vaulted ceiling. "Jamie, David! Jamie, David! Jamie, David! Yes! Yes! Yes!" He pulled his arms down, crossed them at the wrists on his chest and glanced back and forth between the two of them grinning wildly.

Jamie cleared her throat and looked at Brett with wide eyes. "Are you trying to say that you're my father?"

Brett's face suddenly seemed to soften. An awareness came to his eyes, focused, alert and attentive. "Yes, Jamie," he said with a calm clarity. "You are my daughter." He held her gaze and nodded. "I've missed you so very much. I have wanted to know you for so long and now here you are."

Jamie's mouth hung open. She looked deeply into his eyes as his lucidity began to rapidly fade away. He tilted his head quickly from side to side. "Jamie, Jamie, Jamie," he said. "David, David, David. Pray, pray twice a day and then pray thrice on Sunday."

Ralph Nelson Willett

Chapter 5

Jamie walked into her mother's home through the kitchen door. The smell of taco seasoning identified the evening's dinner.

"Hi, Hon," her mother said from behind the stove. She removed the pan of taco meat from the hot burner, to a cold one and turned it off. Jamie set the wooden carving of her as a graduating angel carefully on the dining table, mindful of the fragile tassel. She pulled the one of her singing as a young girl out of a plastic bag and set it beside the first carving.

"What are those?" her mother asked.

Jamie removed her spring jacket as she walked back to the kitchen door and hung it on a coat rack.

"You'll need to see these," Jamie told her as she walked back to the table and sat down in a chair with the carvings placed in front of her.

Carol Ann met Jamie at the table and stood beside her as she looked down at the carvings. She gently picked up the carving of the angel. "Look at this," she said in amazement.

"Be careful with that one. The tassel is very fragile," Jamie told her.

"It's you," Carol Ann said in surprise. She sat in the chair at the end of the table. Jamie slid the other carving towards her. Carol Ann set the angel carving down and picked up the carving of the young girl singing. "This is you, too," she said in quiet amazement. "Who made these?" she asked as she turned the carving upside down, examining it for a maker's mark.

Jamie did not answer. Carol Ann looked away from the carving and at Jamie. "Who made these?" she asked again.

Jamie held her eyes fixed with her mother's but said nothing. "Jamie?" she prompted again.

Jamie looked away and pulled out the first letter from her purse. "Remember a few weeks back when I asked about my father?" Carol Ann was perplexed as to how that would relate to the carvings. "I asked because I received a letter." Jamie laid the letter, still folded, on the table in front of her mother. Carol Ann put the carving down, gave Jamie a worried look and picked it up.

Carol Ann unfolded the pages slowly. Jamie watched as she read the brief note. Carol Ann's eyes clouded over. She did not look at the drawing on the second page. She slowly folded the paper and set it on the table in front of her. Her movements were slow and deliberate as she looked down, pulled her hands back and let them hang by her fingers on the edge of the table.

Jamie waited.

Carol Ann stood and stepped back from the table. "We're having taco's tonight," she said as she walked towards the stove. She stopped in front of the stove, her back to Jamie and stood there long moments without moving.

"Mom," Jamie said. "You need to talk to me." Carol Ann did not move. "Mom?" Jamie prompted again. Carol Ann hung her head and shook it slowly. Jamie walked to the counter by the stove, leaned against it and faced her mother. Jamie could see that her mother was crying. "Mom," she prompted again. "You need to talk to me. There are some things I deserve to know."

Carol Ann wiped her face with the palms of her hands, sniffed and straightened her back. She walked into the living room, sat down on the sofa, folded her hands in her lap and let her head hang down. She stared down at the floor with unfocused eyes. "All this time," she said quietly. "So, did you meet Brett?"

"Yes."

"Did he find you or did you find him?"

"He found me."

"How?"

"I don't know."

"Did he tell you he was your father?"

"Yes."

Carol Ann shook her head side to side slowly. "All these years I kept my promise. I suppose it doesn't matter now. He didn't keep his."

Jamie sat next to her and turned to face her. "Mom," she began. "Tell me about Brett St. James."

"Did he make those carvings?"

"Yes."

Carol Ann pursed her lips and nodded. "So very talented." She looked up at Jamie with a sad face. They held each other's eyes for a moment before Carol Ann nodded slowly and looked down again. Jamie waited as her mother tried to piece together the story she had to tell.

"I loved him," she began. "Did you ever make a mistake so bad that you thought it was going to mess up the rest of your life?" Carol Ann asked quietly.

"Yeah, Mom," Jamie replied. "Everyone has."

"I suppose," her mother answered quietly. She waited a moment and then looked up at Jamie. "Brett St. James and I made promises to each other."

"What promises?"

Carol Ann looked at Jamie's face a moment and then looked down at the floor again. "You're the best thing that could have ever happened to me," she said. "I love you. You know that."

"Yes, Mom," Jamie answered. "I know that. And I love you, too."

"It's hard to believe that you actually met him after all these years."

"Yes," Jamie answered. "He gave me those carving. He has hundreds."

Carol Ann paused as she chose her words carefully to tell the story for the first time in her life. "I've never told anyone about him. That's what we agreed to. I honestly don't know why I'm so upset by it now. It's been over thirty years." She paused before continuing and wiped her eyes one more time. She inhaled deeply and let it out, folded her hands in her lap and began. "I was eighteen and just out of high school. I got a job in the office at St. James Industries. It's called Tashe Industries or something now."

"Tashe International," Jamie corrected.

"OK," her mother responded. She paused a moment. "I was so young and naïve. It was my first job. I was making good money. I wanted to move into my own apartment, so I was putting all my money away. There was so much work there that needed to be done that my boss let me work as many hours as I wanted. A lot of the exec staff worked late too, so since I was there, some of them asked me to help them out occasionally. Mostly just retrieving files or finding something for them. I got a couple of raises and finally got my own apartment. After about a year, Brett St. James noticed me, I mean how I worked. He owned the company.

He inherited it from his grandfather who died just a couple of months after I started there."

Carol Ann paused again. She pulled a tissue from a box on the end table next to her and wiped her nose with it. "He worked in the front office before, but when his grandfather died, he moved into the CEO's office. He must have been around forty at the time." Carol Ann shook her head as she considered that. "No, probably early to mid-thirties. I thought he was a rock star. I'd sit in meetings with him sometimes as his assistant and he was just amazing. Just the way he talked and took control of everything. He seemed so brilliant. He had it all, good looks, brains and charm.

"We spent a lot of time together, but he was married and there was nothing between us except work. I still worked late, getting as many hours in as I could, and Brett came to rely on me being there when he was there. He'd have me type things up for him, get people on the phone, find things for him. It was a great job.

"When I was twenty, there was an executive conference that was being held in Las Vegas. The senior executive assistant had a daughter that was expecting a baby that week, so I was invited to go along in her place. It was all innocent. I had been to off-site meetings before with some of the executives, a couple of times out of town, but this time it was in Vegas and I had never been there. I was just so excited to be going.

"The whole conference was great. I helped out all the execs during the day and then at night while the execs were partying, me and one of the other assistants would go out and find something to do. I was too young to gamble or drink, you had to be twenty-one, so we'd hit the shows and stuff.

"The last night there, Brett wanted all of us to be together, so he had me find a room where we could have our own private party. It took a while, but I found one. It had a staffed bar and food and we even got some entertainment.

"So that night I was busy with the arrangements and when I finally got to sit down, the only seat available was next to Brett, so I sat next to him. There were at least a dozen people there. I can still remember most of their names. It was a lot of fun, everyone was laughing and having a great time. When the meal was served, they poured me a glass of white wine. I wasn't supposed to be drinking, but nobody asked, and I didn't tell. After dinner, I had arranged for some comedian to come in and give us a fifteen-minute set. I can't remember his name, but he was funny.

"Afterwards, people started leaving and Brett and I just stayed and talked. We talked about work and our families and all kinds of stuff. I think I had too much wine, maybe we both did. Then he asked me if I wanted to walk the strip a little bit, so we went out for a walk. We must have walked for about two hours. I was so starstruck with him I didn't even know what time it was when we headed back to the hotel. Then, on the elevator, on the way up to our rooms I kissed him." Carol Ann paused. "It just sort of happened. The elevator opened at my floor, but I didn't get out. I went up to his room. I, uh, you know. It just happened."

Carol Ann puffed her cheeks out as she blew out a breath of air. "It just happened," she repeated. "The next morning, he was very apologetic. He kept saying how sorry he was. He didn't mean for it to happen. He felt a lot more guilty about it than I ever did. He had a wife and a kid. He messed up, and he knew it. I told him not to worry about it. I wasn't going to tell anyone if he didn't. I thought it was all done with then."

Carol Ann bobbed her head up and down in a slow movement as she waded through her memory. Jamie prompted her, "Is that when you found out you were pregnant with me?"

Carol Ann did not look up. "Yes. That's what happened. He was terrified of losing his wife and son. He was so afraid that his wife would find out. He was shaking when I talked to him about it. That whole rock star thing faded pretty quickly then for me. He had no idea what to do. I quit working late so I could avoid being alone with him. A couple of weeks later he called me into his office and he closed the door. He was still scared. That's when he made me an offer. He said that if I could keep his name out of it, he'd be sure you were taken care of financially. He'd give me a generous living expense and set you up with a college fund. He offered to have his lawyer put everything in writing, but I told him it wasn't necessary. Looking back, I see that I was pretty naïve but we both promised not to tell anyone anything about it and we wouldn't have contact with each other again. And that was it. We didn't."

Carol Ann looked up at Jamie. "And that's what happened. We never saw each other again. He kept his word. I kept mine. Your whole college was paid for by him. We got to live in this house because he paid for it. He set us up with a bank account and put enough money in to keep us going for several years. You know that full ride scholarship from the Ohio Women's Advancement Foundation you won because your essay was so good?"

Jamie nodded.

"That foundation was set up just to be sure you had your college all paid for. No one else ever received a scholarship from them and never will."

Jamie's mouth hung open. All of her college expenses had been covered, but she had not known what the foundation was about or who ran it. She had only counted herself lucky. The only interaction she ever had with them was to send them letters at the end of each school year as a thank you, letting them know how her degree was coming and how much she appreciated the scholarship award. She shook her head to clear her thoughts. "So, he paid you hush money," Jamie said coldly.

Carol Ann snapped her head up and looked at her wide eyed. "No. It wasn't like that," she said. "I didn't want to break up his family. We both made a mistake, and he wanted to be sure his daughter was taken care of. He was a good man."

"It still sounds like he paid you hush money."

"I know how it looks. But that's not the way it was." Carol Ann relaxed and looked back down. She paused and then continued. "I quit working for St. James right after. I haven't seen or heard from him since. Before you showed me the letter and carvings, I thought he had forgotten all about us, but he's obviously seen you a couple of times."

There was a brief silence before Carol Ann spoke again. "So, you got to meet him," she stated flatly.

"Yes."

"How is he?"

"He's insane."

Carol Ann looked into Jamie's eyes. "What do you mean?"

"He's lost his mind," Jamie told her. "He isn't all there. He can't hold a conversation with you. He repeats the same thing over and over. He's living by himself in an old church in Amison, a small town south of Columbus. That's where I went to meet him. He's made hundreds of these carvings. A lot of them are of me. He gave these two to me." She pointed at the carvings on the table.

"What happened?" her mother asked.

"Apparently, he lost his mind after his wife died," Jamie told her. "But you know what's really spooky? He knew where I lived. He was able to send me two letters, but he can't talk like a normal human."

"What do you mean by 'lost his mind'? Carol Ann asked.

"Well, he's not right. He keeps repeating things over and over. Like when he saw me for the first time, he was hitting himself in the head and saying 'stupid, stupid, stupid'. He knew who I was, but he acted as if he didn't know if I was real or not. He touched me like he was checking to see if I was really there. Then just before I was kicked out, he yells, 'pray, pray, twice a day and then pray thrice on Sunday'. It was really weird."

"Who kicked you out?" her mother interrupted.

"People from town. They didn't know who I was and didn't want me snooping around. Later, I saw him walking downtown back to the church with bags of groceries. I tried to talk to him then, but he wouldn't even look at me. He kept saying, 'not real, not real'. Last Saturday, when I saw him, I met his son, David, at the church. Brett asked David if I was real and then he touched me to be sure. Then he gets all excited and kept saying my name over and over again. And he kept saying 'pray, pray, twice a day and then pray thrice on Sunday'. That isn't just not normal, that's way over the edge."

Carol Ann looked down somberly. "That's too bad," she said. "I was in love with him at one time."

"Mom, why did you have to keep him a secret for this long? You could have told me."

Carol Ann did not look up. "Because that's what I agreed to do. We made promises to each other. I always try to keep my word. I didn't want to cause any trouble. I didn't know his wife had died. Maybe had I known I could have told you."

"What kind of trouble did you think there'd be?" Jamie asked her.

"I don't know. But what difference would it had made? I kept my word, and he kept his. I always *wanted* to tell you."

"Then why didn't you?"

Carol Ann looked up into Jamie's face. "Jamie," she began. "I love you. But there are things in my life that I was just too embarrassed to talk about. I should have known better. I was so young and naïve at the time. I fell in love with a married man and nearly ruined both our lives because of it."

"Don't you think he had something to do with it? I think you could have made a great case for sexual harassment. He was your boss, and he took advantage of you."

Carol Ann shook her head. "No, Jamie," she said. "Please don't think that's how it was. Nothing improper happened until that one night. It was just a mistake. I wanted him so badly that night. We both screwed up, and we both knew it."

Jamie leaned back in her chair and brushed her hair back from her face. Her mother looked sad and defeated. "Mom," Jamie said. "I just wanted to know who my father was."

"I know."

There was a long silence. "You going to be OK?" Jamie asked.

"Yeah. I'm fine." Carol Ann hesitated for a moment, then added, "You wanted to know who your father was, but I made a promise and I wanted to let the past stay in the past. Now I guess I'm kind of glad it's over."

"Mom, I really don't understand what the big deal is. So, what if my father was some big shot? What difference does it make? He's certainly not a big shot now."

Carol Ann shook her head. "It wasn't about being a big shot. He was married and neither one of us wanted to ruin it. But then, aren't there some things in your life that you'd rather not dredge up?"

"Yeah," she answered, "but nothing like this. I think I would want my daughter to know who her father was."

The sadness in Carol Ann's eyes was replaced with an angry tension. "So, you've got stuff that you wouldn't want to share with me, but you're upset with me because I don't want to discuss something that happened thirty years ago. Why do you think you have a right to do that?"

"Because he's my father," Jamie shot back. "I have a right to know who my father is."

"So now you know!" Carol Ann retorted angrily. "Now what're you going to do with it? Huh? You've found out that your father is crazy, and your mother isn't perfect. Nice. Now what're you going to do with all that?"

Jamie looked down at the floor and forced herself to release the tension in her body. Her mother stared at her with angry eyes. Jamie had not intended to make her angry, and she still did not understand why her mother should be so upset at her. "Mom, I'm sorry," she said.

Slowly, Carol Ann let go of the anger that had been building up. She sat back in her chair, slouching slightly.

After several moments Carol Ann asked quietly, "So what are you going to do now that you know?"

Jamie shrugged her shoulders. She had not thought beyond confronting her mother with what she knew. "I don't know," she said. "I can't have a relationship with him. He's several bricks short of a full load. And besides, I suspect that the townspeople don't want me around. They keep asking me if I am a reporter or if I work for the state. I don't know what that's supposed to mean." She sat quietly for a moment and then added, "I guess there really isn't a reason to do anything. It doesn't make a difference at all anymore."

Jamie looked up and Carol Ann locked eyes with her. "No," Carol Ann said. "It doesn't."

Chapter 6

Jamie let her eyes rest on the carving of the singing girl she had placed on her office desk. She was fascinated by it. Was it the carving itself that fascinated her or was it the man who created it? As a little girl she would fantasize about the father she had never met. He was tall, strong and handsome. She knew that someday he would walk into her mother's front door and tell her why he had never been there for her. He would tell her that he was in the jungles of Africa or on some secret mission, or he was being held prisoner in some far away exotic land only to escape with his life by his wits and martial arts skills. He would be smart, smarter than her teachers, even smarter than the president of the United States.

But the reality was that her father was insane, was suffering from dementia or perhaps had a stroke. He was unable to communicate with her in any meaningful way. The man he once was, the man she never knew, was gone. Her childish fantasies crashed all around her.

Several times she had considered driving back to Amison to see Brett St. James again, but why bother? Trying to meet with a man she did not know, someone who could not hold a conversation with her, made the two-hour drive in both directions seem pointless.

Her desk phone rang, shaking her out of her thoughts. She put her headset on and answered it. "This is Jamie," she said.

"Hi, is this Jamie Fulton?" a man's voice asked.

"Yes," she answered, "how can I help you?"

"My name is Curt Linden. I knew your father," the man told her. "I used to work with him at Tashe International back when it was known as St. James Industries."

Why would anyone want to call her about Brett? "Ok," she said, "Brett St. James?"

"Yes. I'd like to talk to you if I may."

"OK," Jamie replied. "I have some time. Go ahead."

"Please," the man said. "I'd like to meet in person. Can we do that?"

Jamie held her breath as objections raced through her mind. No, we can't. I don't know you. What could you possibly have to tell me that you couldn't tell me over the phone? There isn't a single thing you could tell me that would make a difference.

The man recognized her hesitation. "There's a restaurant two blocks over from your office called Callub's. Can we meet there?"

"Why?" she asked.

"Because there are some things I'd like to tell you about your father. Some things I think you'd like to know," the man said.

Jamie considered her answer carefully. The restaurant was very public, and the wait staff was familiar with her. If she was going to meet someone she did not know, then it was probably one of the better choices of location. Perhaps she could take someone with her. "OK," she said as she checked the clock on her PC. It was already a quarter past eleven. "What time would you like to meet? Would twelve thirty today be OK?"

"That would be perfect," he replied. "I'll meet you there. See you then."

"Wait!" Jamie nearly shouted into the phone trying to catch him before he hung up. "How will I know you? How will I know what you look like?"

"I know what you look like," the man said. "I think I can find you OK. I'll be the one with the wheelchair. I'll see you there."

He disconnected, and Jamie's line immediately returned to a dial tone. Jamie pulled her headset off slowly and put it back in its charging cradle. How did this man know what she looked like? The name, Curt Linden, was not familiar to her. How did he know who she was? How could he know her direct office line? How did he know anything at all about her?

A knot was building in her stomach. Meeting someone she did not know for lunch was not something she, as an introvert, would normally do. She needed to take someone else with her. Teresa? Michael? Rachael? Who could step in in case of trouble? Phil. He would go. No one would mess with that big guy.

Phil Redhawk had become a friend since he began working in the same office with her two months prior. He was roughly the same age as her. Tall, muscular, and friendly, his Native American heritage on his father's side gave him a rich skin tone. They took their breaks at the same time in the office's small break room. He and Jamie had been getting to know each other as they talked over coffee.

She walked over to Phil's cube. His back was to her. He leaned in as he examined a spreadsheet on his computer. "Hey, Phil," she said.

Phil turned his chair to face her. "Hey, Jamie," he said with a smile. "What's up?"

"Can you come with me for a twelve-thirty lunch meeting at Callub's today?"

"I already have a meeting at twelve-thirty. What kind of meeting are you having at Callub's?"

"I need to meet someone I don't know, and I'd rather not go alone?"

Phil cocked his head almost imperceptibly to one side. His eyebrows lowered as he looked at her. "Who are you meeting?"

"Someone called me. He says he knows my father, and he has something to tell me about him. He wants to meet at Callub's."

Phil looked down at the floor for a moment. He shook his head slowly. "I can't get out of my meeting. Can you postpone it?

"Maybe. I don't know."

"Can anyone else go with you?"

"I haven't asked anyone else," Jamie said. "He says he's in a wheelchair. I just don't like the idea of going by myself."

"Then don't," Phil told her with a shrug. "It's probably just some gossip anyhow. Why bother?"

"It's not like that," Jamie told him. "I never knew who my father was, then I get a letter from some guy named Brett St. James with a note that says he can tell me about him. I met him at some church in Amison."

"Where's Amison?"

"The other side of Columbus. I went there…"

"Alone?" Phil interrupted.

"Yeah. It was in a church, so I figured it would be OK. Anyhow, I met some guy there that wasn't right. There was something wrong with him. It was like he was mentally handicapped or something. I don't know how to describe it. He was just weird. But the scary part is: he knew who I was, knew my name. I've never seen that guy in my life. Then some people threw me out of the church. I didn't get a chance to try to talk with him."

"Threw you out?"

"Oh, yeah," she said. "Some big guy and an older woman. She asked me if I was a reporter. That was weird."

"Did you find out anything about your father?" Phil asked.

"Not then. The guy at the church was acting weird and all. He couldn't tell me anything. I went back the next day and stopped at the restaurant in town to see if someone knew if he had a guardian or someone else I could talk to. After they found out I actually went inside the church, they practically chased me out of town then, too. But someone told me that his son comes to visit every other Saturday, so I went back and met his son. He was expecting me. When we went in to see his father, that's when the guy told us we were brother and sister. His son had never heard of me either. That guy is my father."

"Can he prove it?"

"My mother confirmed it."

"So now someone else wants to tell you some family gossip," Phil stated matter-of-factly. He looked away as he considered it and then looked back. "I'd say postpone it."

Jamie nodded. "I'll think about it. It's at Callub's so it should be fine, but I was kind of hoping you could go with me."

"Postpone it," Phil said. "I'd love to go."

~~~

She vacillated. Should she go or not? Her curiosity overcame her caution and she decided to go as the clock read twelve thirty.

She walked into the restaurant fifteen minutes late. As she walked in the door, she looked around and locked eyes with an elderly man in a wheelchair sitting alone at a table. He nodded, smiled and gave her a short wave of his hand.

"Hi, Jamie," he said as she approached the table. "I'm glad you could make it."

"Hi, Mr. Linden," Jamie said as she offered him her hand.

"Please," he said as he shook it, "call me Curt." He motioned for her to take a seat across the table from him. "I was just starting to think that you changed your mind," he said as Jamie seated herself.

"Yeah," she replied. "I almost *didn't* come. So, how do you know me and what's this about?"

Linden chuckled. "Very much like your father: straight to business," he said. "Do you mind if we order first? I haven't eaten anything yet today."

"Sure," Jamie replied as she picked up the menu off the table in front of her. She tried to relax and focus on the menu but struggled to keep her attention on it. She closed it and put it back down on the table in front of her. "I eat here all the time. I know what I want," she told him. Linden smiled and then signaled the waitress.

After taking their orders, the waitress walked away with their menus. Jamie folded her hands and rested them on top of the table in front of her. Linden did the same, mirroring Jamie's movements.

"What did you want to see me about?" Jamie asked him.

"I understand that you've met your father," he said.

"Yes," she replied. "Brett St. James. How did you hear that?"

"Some townspeople. I worked with Brett for many years, since just before he took over the company from his grandfather. I retired from St. James Industries about a year before his wife died. I can honestly say that he and I were best of friends." He paused as if he was expecting her to comment.

"OK," Jamie said, prompting him to continue.

"What do you know about your mother and Brett?"

"Just that they had a one-nighter in Vegas and that I was a result of that."

"That's it?" Linden asked with surprise in his voice.

"Well, no," she responded thoughtfully. "I know that he set my mom up with some kind of account and set up a special scholarship to pay for my college."

"Yes," Linden said. "There were only three people that knew about all this: Brett, your mother and me. It was kept pretty well hidden from everyone else. The reason I knew about it was because I was his best friend. And since I was also the financial officer of the company, I helped him set up and hide the accounts. He was a very religious man, going to church every Sunday and all. He had a lot of guilt because he cheated on his wife."

"OK," Jamie prompted again as she suppressed an urge to roll her eyes. This was information that she already knew.

"Your father only had one child with his wife Rene, a son. I think he always wanted a daughter. He followed you as closely as he could ever since you were a baby. He attended some of the concerts you sang in when you were in your school choir. He attended your high school and college graduations. He would sometimes go to your church on Sundays, just so he could get a glimpse of you. He was so proud of you even though he never actually met you. He always *wanted* to meet you but because of the agreement he had with your mother, he couldn't. He was like that, he always kept his word."

Jamie nodded at him. "So, he didn't want his wife to find out he had an affair. I get it."

"Yeah. That's the really simple answer, but yeah. He really loved Rene," Linden said. "He had so much guilt over what he did that it almost sent him over the edge then. Most other guys would have either blocked out the guilt or chalked it up as just another conquest and moved on with their lives, but not Brett. Then about seven years ago, Rene found out she had breast cancer. She fought it for as long as she could and died two years later."

Linden paused and looked down. "He really loved Rene. He was a good man. He had so much guilt over what happened with your mother. He never really forgave himself. Then when she got cancer, he put everything he had into her, emotionally that is. He seemed to think that God was punishing him for the affair by giving Rene cancer, so he did everything he could. He could pay for the best medical treatments and hospitals that were available anywhere, but it just wasn't enough. He let his son handle the day-to-day operations of the company. I think you met David?"

Jamie nodded. "Yes. We've met."

"My legs were getting bad," he said as he reached down and tapped one of the wheelchair wheels, "so I decided to retire early. That was just before Rene got sick, so I wasn't much help with the company. Everyone expected that Brett was going to return to work after she died. He was sixty when she passed. He was in good shape physically and he loved his company, but he never returned. He stayed by that church all the time. He'd spend hours next to Rene's grave just moping.

"After her death, Brett just went downhill from there. He was so depressed that he could hardly function. David found a local doctor there in Amison to help take care of him, but he just kept getting worse. He started doing those pictures and then a little later started making those carvings, one after another after another. They just kept coming. I think it was a way for him to relax and take his mind off Rene for a while. David had some people from town keep him stocked with wood and clean up after him. You've seen the carvings, haven't you?"

"Yes," Jamie said. "There's a lot of me."

"You, yes," Linden said. "There were only a handful of Rene, some animals, flowers and stuff, but none of David oddly enough. David never knew anything about you, not until the day you showed up at the church."

"Brett sent me a letter asking me to meet him at the church."

"Jamie," Linden said as he bowed his head, "that's part of why I wanted to meet with you. I have a confession to make." He paused, looked down, then looked up sheepishly. "I wrote the letter."

Jamie's eyes opened wide and she leaned away from him. "You?" she asked. "Why did you do that?"

"He wasn't capable of writing you a letter," Linden told her. "I try to go to visit him almost every week when the weather is good. He can draw those beautiful pictures and make wonderful carvings, but he can't put words together. Once in a great while he can say a sentence or two but that's it."

"But why would you do that?"

"Because of the carvings. So many of them are of you. I didn't realize it at first but then it hit me that they were of you. He gave me several of them. He's my friend. I wanted to help him out. There was no reason for him not to get to know you now. There's still a lot of Brett left in him. I don't know how much longer he has. He should at least get to *meet* his daughter before he passes."

Jamie's stomach knotted at hearing that the letter was not from Brett. She had been lied to. She could think of no reason to forge a letter. Why wouldn't Linden send the letter himself?

"Look, Jamie," he said, sensing her rising anger. "I probably should have sent the letters from me. It may not have been the smartest thing I've ever done but I'm really looking for your help. I'm stuck in this wheelchair. I can only visit him when he's outside. There's no way for me to get in the church anymore. Jamie, I think there's something going on. I need someone's help. Would you have been willing to help me if you hadn't met him first? I'm actually hoping that you'd be willing to, now that you have."

She narrowed her eyes at him. "What do you think is going on?"

"I think Brett is either being drugged or poisoned."

Jamie's jaw dropped as her mind raced.

"Early on, Brett signed a power of attorney and medical power of attorney over to David. Brett was going downhill fast. He had sunk down into a depression so far that I thought we should hospitalize him then. David refused. Now that David had taken over the company, he renamed it to Tashe International. I've no idea where he came up with the name, 'Tashe'. Now, he's taking the company public. The IPO, Initial Public Offering, is scheduled in a couple of months."

"I still don't understand," Jamie told him. "Why would someone want to poison him?"

"When the company goes public, David is going to be a very wealthy man, much wealthier than Brett ever was, and that's saying a lot. But as long as Brett is alive there is potential for messing all that up."

"Why?"

"Because technically, Brett still owns one hundred percent of it. If the word reached the press that he had a mental breakdown, then that could affect the IPO. It could put questions in the minds of the investors. When there are questions, it could affect the IPO by billions."

Jamie tilted her head at him.

"That's billions with a B," he added.

Jamie nodded and looked down in contemplation.

Linden continued. "Brett never wanted to take the company public. He built that company up to what it is today from what his grandfather left him. He was very good. He liked the fact that the company was more like family than a business. He knew most of the employees by name. But David isn't so sharp. I worked alongside of him since he got out of college. All David thinks about is how much money he can make. He never steps out on the factory floor or wants anything to do with the people that work for him. I retired before Brett checked out, but David hasn't changed."

"Is that why the townspeople asked me if I was a reporter?"

"Probably. I think David told them to watch out for reporters and run them off."

"They also asked if I was from the state."

"I suspect David told them to keep anyone from the state away, too. I'd bet there's some cash being floated around to make sure everyone is chased off. He doesn't want any state mental health workers showing up, for sure. If they did, they'd want to put Brett into some treatment facility. If Brett got better, then the IPO would fail. I don't think anyone expected a daughter would show up. That surprised everyone."

"They didn't know I was his daughter," Jamie said coldly. "*I* didn't know I was his daughter."

"Did you show them the letter?" Linden asked.

"Yes," she answered. "I gave them a copy when I met some people in the restaurant."

"I think that's why David let you see him. He recognized Brett's drawing. But I don't think they knew what to do with you."

"Then you sent the second letter?"

"Yes. I felt you needed a bit more prompting. I'm pretty sure that they called David to let him know you showed up and gave them the letter. That made David curious. I think he wanted to know who you were, so he told them to let him know right away if you showed up again."

"So, if Brett suddenly got better, then David would lose money?" Jamie asked.

"That's right," Linden answered. "You've complicated things. Just the fact that David has discovered that Brett has a daughter he didn't know about, probably scared the heck out of him. He's got to be wondering what you want. Are you after the money?"

"That never occurred to me," Jamie said flatly. "I was never after his money. I didn't even know there *was* money when this all started. I just don't think that way."

"I understand," he replied. "But David does. He's got to be wondering if you could mess up the IPO."

"Why would I want to do that?" she asked. "I only wanted to know who my father was."

"Just because you exist, it could create questions in the minds of the investors. Questions mean less money."

Jamie leaned back in her chair. "So, what am I supposed to do? I can't *not* exist?"

"Don't be so sure of that."

"What?" Jamie asked in surprise.

"I don't know what David is capable of. So, I'm trying to tell you to be careful."

Jamie's eyes blinked rapidly. Her heart rate picked up. "Are you saying he'd kill me?"

"Like I said, I don't know what he's capable of. He can be cruel to people sometimes. He's not known for wise choices."

"Well, I don't think that's going to be a problem. I don't think I'll be going back to see Brett. There's no point. He may know who I am but there's no way I can get to know him. There's no way I can have any type of relationship with him, not in his condition. But I've got a question for you: How did you find me? How did you know where to send me those letters?"

Linden looked down and cleared his throat before looking up again. "I hired a private investigator," he said meekly.

"Why?" Jamie asked. "Why me? There's nothing I can do about anything. What's the point?" Jamie paused a moment, then asked more quietly. "What else did you find out about me?"

"That was it," Linden said. "I just needed to get ahold of you."

"I'm not comfortable with this."

"I'm sorry," Linden said, "but I needed to find you. You may be the only one that can help. I knew about you from everything Brett had told me, but a few years had passed, and you moved into your own house and all. I didn't know where you were."

"Help with what?"

"I'm Brett's friend, but there are some things that I obviously can't do, like go inside that church. It's not handicap accessible. You can. I'd like to check to see if my suspicions are correct. To start with, I'd like to prove that Brett is or isn't being poisoned, then I'd like to get him some help, some real help."

"I'm not planning to go see him again," Jamie said quietly.

"That's what I thought. That's why I wanted to talk to you."

"If all you want to do is find out if he's being poisoned, then why not call the cops or something?" Jamie asked him.

"I did that," Linden answered. "I asked the cops to stop by and check things out and then I called the state mental health department. Nothing changed. I don't even know if they went out to see him. Maybe they didn't or maybe they did and didn't see anything wrong or maybe," he paused, "maybe David paid them off."

The waitress returned to their table with their orders and placed it in front of them. Jamie leaned back in her seat and stared at her food. Linden unwrapped the paper napkin from around his silverware. He began spreading jelly on the toast.

"What is it that you think that I'm supposed to do?" Jamie asked him.

"Help me find out what's going on with him. Let's prove if my suspicions are correct or not. Let's be sure if he's being poisoned. Let's find out if his mental state is natural or not."

"How am I supposed to do that?"

"I'm not sure," Linden responded. "But I think you can start by trying to get to know him a little better. Look around the church and see if you can see anything unusual: maybe pill bottles or something."

"I'll have to think about it," Jamie said.

"What's there to think about?" Linden asked.

"When I met him, he just seemed crazy, not ill. Physically, he looked fine. He didn't look poisoned to me. I met his son, David. He was a nice guy. I just can't see him trying to poison his own father."

"I understand," Linden said as he put his fork down on the table. He stared down at his food for a moment, then said, "David *is* a nice guy, but sometimes he does some dumb things. I can understand why you may not want to be involved, but I think you may be the only one to be able to do this."

"Why not send your private investigator?" Jamie asked with a hint of sarcasm.

"I did. The townspeople ran him off the same way they did to you. He went back and snuck into the church one night but then Brett chased him off with a wooden club. He just couldn't get anywhere with it. That's why I think you may be the only one to be able to do this. He knows you. He *wants* to see you."

Jamie unwrapped her silverware and poked at her salad with her fork. "Fine," she said. "OK. I'll do it."

Chapter 7

Jamie could see Brett sitting on a garden bench in the little cemetery from where she parked in front of the church. She locked her car and walked across the lawn. The bench was made out of decorative wrought iron. It was pushed back against the knee-high green wrought iron fencing. Brett sat hunched over with his elbows on his thighs. He faced the pink granite headstone directly in front of him as he gesticulated with his hands as if he were talking with someone. As Jamie approached, she heard Brett speaking softly. She read the name on the stone, Rene St. James.

Jamie stood behind Brett on the outside of the fence and listened for a moment. Brett's words were whispered, mumbled and unintelligible.

"Hi, Brett," Jamie said quietly.

Brett turned slowly, looking over his right shoulder at her. He blinked hard twice and then slowly turned away to face the headstone again.

"Brett, it's me, Jamie," she told him.

"Real?" Brett asked without turning.

"Yes. I'm real," she answered. "Do you mind if I come in?"

"Jamie, Jamie, Jamie," he said sadly.

"Can I come sit by you for a moment?"

Brett shrugged his shoulders. Jamie walked a few paces to the opening in the fence, came around and sat down on the far side of him. She put her arm around his back and hugged him to her.

"Jamie, Jamie, Jamie," he said. There was sadness in his voice.

"What's wrong, Brett," she asked.

"Pray, pray, twice a day and then pray thrice on Sunday."

Jamie released him and sat upright. She folded her hands in her lap and looked forward with Brett towards the headstone. Nothing was said for long moments until Brett said, "I'm sorry."

"What are you sorry for, Brett?" Jamie asked him.

"I'm sorry, Rene," he said. Jamie realized that he was not apologizing to her but to Rene. "This is," he began and then cleared his throat. "This is Jamie. My daughter." There was a long silence. He then said, "She's a good girl." He then turned to look up at Jamie. "This is my wife, Rene." Tears

The Legacy

were welling up in his eyes. "Please say hi," he said as he turned slowly back toward the stone.

It was awkward. Should she say hello? Should she let it pass? Brett turned again to her. His eyes were pleading. Jamie looked at the stone. "Hi, Rene," she said.

Brett began talking to the stone again. "I'm sorry. I didn't mean for it to happen. Please forgive me. This is my daughter." He hung his head and began to weep. Tears fell in streams to the grass below.

Jamie wrapped her arm around his back again and pulled him in tightly against her. His entire body trembled with the sobs. Jamie held him until he began to calm. "God is punishing me," he said.

"Oh, no, sweetie," she said. "God isn't punishing you. Why would you think that?"

"He took Rene away from me because of what I did." His body trembled as tears began to fall again.

"Brett, I'm sorry Rene died," she said. "But she didn't die because God wants to punish you. Rene died because it was her time. That's all. You just feel sad because she's not here with you right now. I know you miss her but I'm sure you're going to see her again."

"Pray, pray twice a day and then pray thrice on Sunday," he said softly. "Every day, I ask God to forgive me. Every day." He then whispered, "pray, pray twice a day and then pray thrice on Sunday."

93

"Well, Sweetie," she said gently. "God has already forgiven you. You don't have to keep saying you're sorry every day."

Brett looked up at her. He appeared confused. "David said I must pray every day," he said. He looked towards the stone again. "Every day… every day… every day…," he whispered.

An angry shout came from a woman walking rapidly towards them. "Hey!" Brett and Jamie turned to see the same small woman and large man who had forced her out of the church the first time. "What do you think you're doing?" she shouted. Jamie stood and turned to face her. Brett stood and stepped beside her. "You have no reason to be here!" she shouted as she scowled and pointed an accusing finger at her. The woman stopped on the other side of the bench and fence. The large man caught up and stood beside her.

"He's my father," Jamie told her calmly. "I just want to talk with him."

"You need to leave! Now!" the woman said angrily as she swept her arm towards the road.

"I just want to talk with him a few more minutes."

The woman scowled at her. "Ken," she said, "help her leave."

The man stepped over the fence and faced Jamie. He took a step towards her. Jamie flinched and stepped back as he reached for her.

The Legacy

In one swift circular movement, Brett raised his open hand and swung it down hard, hitting the bridge of Ken's nose with the palm of his hand. Ken staggered back and fell to a seated position on the ground. He was dazed as he fought to bring everything into focus. Blood began to trickle from his nose. He shook his head, trying to clear the cobwebs. The woman's mouth hung open in surprise. Brett took one step towards the man on the ground, clenched his fist and held them out just inches from his sides, curling them inward. Every muscle was taut as if ready to explode. He leaned in towards the man, his face contorted in anger. "Ahhhhhh!!!!" Brett screamed at him. He took another step forward. The man scrambled back and fumbled his way to his feet. "Ahhhhhh!!!" Brett screamed at him again as he took another step towards him. The man turned and took several steps away from Brett before quickly stepping over the fence. He stumbled to his knees and stood up again. He was wide-eyed as he watched to see if Brett was going to come after him.

The woman began to say something. Brett turned towards her, his fist still clenched by his sides. He took a step closer to her and screamed, "Ahhhhh!!!" The woman quickly moved to stand behind Ken. She grabbed his arm. They were both gape-jawed.

Brett leaned in towards them. He had taken a body builder pose, with his arms flexing by his sides. He was breathing heavily through his nose and glowered angrily at them.

The woman regained her composure. "I'm calling David right now!" she yelled at Jamie. "You don't belong here." She turned and began walking away at a pace that was just shy of a jog. Ken scrambled to keep up with her.

95

Brett visibly relaxed and faced Jamie. Jamie looked at him in stunned amazement. She would have never expected Brett to attack anyone like that. His movements had been nearly athletic in their precision. He smiled at her and sat down again on the bench. With a flick of his hand he motioned Jamie to join him.

Jamie cautiously moved to sit next to him again. "Jamie, Jamie, Jamie," he said as he grinned at her.

"Wow," Jamie said as she tried to get over her internal shock. "I didn't expect that."

Brett wrapped his arm around her back and pulled her into a side hug. He released her, put his elbows on his thighs again and faced Rene's headstone. "Ha!" he said to the stone. He grinned broadly.

"I," she said. "I hope you don't get into trouble for that."

"Ha!" he replied gleefully.

They sat in silence for several moments. Jamie's hands were shaking from the encounter but she tried not to let it show.

"Uh, Brett," Jamie began. "I came here to ask you something."

Brett turned his face up to her.

"I wanted to know if you take any medicine."

The smile faded slowly from Brett's face. He turned back to the stone. His sad gaze returned. He said slowly in a quiet soft voice, "Pray, pray twice a day and then pray thrice on

Sunday." He sat up straight. With a movement that was slow, appearing almost overly cautious, he reached into his right pocket and produced a small white bottle. He cupped the bottle in two hands, looked at her and held it out to Jamie as if it were a baby bird. He extended his hands slowly to her.

Jamie took the bottle from him, trying to mimic the care Brett had taken. It was a small, square, white bottle with a protective cap on it. It appeared to be a prescription drug but there was no prescription tag on it. She gently shook the bottle. It was intended to hold sixty pills, but it was empty. Coznephidone. She had never heard of it before. She pulled out her cell phone and took a picture of the bottle's label.

Brett was looking at her guiltily. "How often do you take this?" she asked him.

Brett shrugged. "Pray, pray twice a day and then pray thrice on Sunday." His answer did not make sense. She wondered if Brett was capable of answering her questions. She focused her attention on the bottle again.

She snapped up to look into Brett's face. "Brett," she began. "Do you take these when you pray?

Brett smiled. "Pray, pray," he said brightly.

"Where do you pray at?" Brett pointed at the church. "Can you show me?"

Brett nodded. He faced the pink granite stone and said, "I'll be right back. I need to show my daughter where to pray."

He stood and held his hand out for Jamie. Jamie took it and stood with him. He led her by the hand into the side door of the church. He walked her to the front of the sanctuary and they stood in front of the altar. He pointed at a padded kneeling bench in front of the large ornate altar.

"You pray here?" she asked.

"Pray, pray twice a day and then pray thrice on Sunday."

Jamie approached the altar and examined it. It was just over waist-high to her. The top was covered with a white cloth that was flush to the front and back edges of the table but overhung the sides by several inches. Each end of the cloth was embroidered with a purple cross. The kneeling bench was designed for two people to kneel side by side in front of the altar. Jamie checked the altar's front, sides and behind it.

Not seeing anything unusual, Jamie stepped back to stand shoulder to shoulder with Brett. "Can you show me how you pray?" she asked him.

He looked at her confused. "Jamie?" he asked.

"Please," she said. "Show me how you pray."

Brett looked at the altar. He hesitated a moment and then slowly approached it. He put his hands on the edge of the altar top and knelt on the kneeling bench. He folded his hands and rested them against the edge of the altar's top. He lowered his forehead against his thumbs. Jamie watched as he remained there, silently praying for a few moments. He then raised his head upwards towards the large wooden cross hanging on the wall at the back of the stage, unclasped his hands and reached them out towards both sides of the altar. In a movement that betrayed years of practice, he put his fingers on the heads of the two cherubs to either side of him and pushed in gently. There was an audible pop. He reached down in front of his knees, retrieved something and stiffened his back straight.

Jamie rushed in to see what he was holding in front of him. He was opening a small white bottle. "Oh my gosh," Jamie said in surprise. She took the bottle from him and shook it. It sounded and felt as if there were a lot of pills in it. Brett looked up at her as she opened the bottle. The pills were white tablets. They looked very similar to plain aspirin except that there were two intersecting lines dividing them into quarter sections. The number twenty-nine etched in the side of each pill.

She looked down and examined the small drawer that the bottle had been hidden in. It was just big enough to hold the bottle of pills. She gently pushed it in. It was spring loaded, and it clicked into place when she closed it.

She looked at Brett. "Can you open that again?"

Brett faced the altar again, reached out, touched the two cherubs and pushed gently in. The drawer snapped out again.

Jamie was stunned. "Oh, my gosh, Brett. Do you take a pill every time you pray?"

Brett shrugged. "Pray, pray twice a day and then pray thrice on Sunday."

"So, do you pray in the morning?" she asked. Brett nodded. "And you pray at night?" Again, Brett nodded. "Do you pray at noon?"

"Pray, pray twice a day and then pray thrice on Sunday," he answered.

"So, you take two of these pills a day and then three on Sunday." She stated it as a fact to him. He nodded.

Jamie looked over the pill bottle again. "Did you pray this morning?" she asked him.

Brett hung his head and then shook it guiltily as if he expected Jamie to be angry with him. "No," he said.

"So, you didn't pray this morning," she stated flatly. "That's why you are able to talk to me today but couldn't the last two times I was here. This drug is messing you up. When you stop taking it, you start getting better and you can at least talk to people."

Jamie held the bottle up at eye level and looked it over again. She put it back in the hidden drawer, snapped it shut and helped Brett to stand again.

She began walking slowly towards the vestibule, deep in thought. Brett walked beside her looking down at her with a worried look on his face. They were halfway to the rear of the sanctuary when the church door snapped open. Doc rushed in with Ken following behind. Ken had wiped the blood from his face. Pieces of tissue extended out from each nostril.

"What are you doing here?" Doc demanded.

"I'm talking to my father," Jamie answered with defiance.

"You know you're not supposed to be here when David isn't here," he said angrily as he approached her. He stopped inches from her face.

"No," she answered. "I didn't know that."

"Well, you're not," he said. He pointed at the door. "You need to leave now!"

"I was just leaving," she said as she tried to sidestep him.

He moved to block her way again. "You broke his nose," he hissed as he pointed at Ken.

"I didn't break his nose," Jamie said incredulously.

"Get out!" Doc demanded. "Do not come back here unless David is with you. Do you understand me?"

Jamie did not answer. She sidestepped him again and moved past him.

"If I see you here again, I'll have you arrested," he said loudly.

Brett stepped up close to Doc and looked down at the smaller man threateningly. Doc swore at him and pushed him back. "Knock it off!" he told Brett.

Jamie turned to look at Brett. His face was beginning to show anger again. She was afraid that he might explode and attack Doc. "Brett," she said loudly to him. "I'll come back and see you later." Brett's face softened. His chest lowered.

"No, you won't!" Doc shouted after her. "Not without David!"

Jamie had reached the outside door where Ken appeared to be standing guard. She stepped around him and put her hand on the push bar when Brett shouted out to her, "Pray, pray twice a day and then pray thrice on Sunday!" She stopped to look over her shoulder at him. Doc was standing in front of him so that Brett had to peer over his shoulder. He raised one arm straight up with a finger pointing skyward. He held his chin up and looked directly at the ceiling. That, thought Jamie, is not the stance of an insane man. That is a pose of triumph.

"Thank you, Brett," she said loud enough for Bret to hear her. Brett looked down at her standing at the door and smiled. She gave him a quick wave goodbye and left the church.

Chapter 8

Jamie's cell rang as she parked her car in her mother's driveway. She left the car running as she answered it. It was David.

"Jamie," he began, "what were you doing at the church?"

"I just wanted to stop and see my father," she told him.

There was a hesitation before he spoke again. "Jamie, I don't want you going there unless I'm there."

"What's the problem?"

"The last time you were there he was agitated for a week. I can't have that. Do you understand? I don't want you seeing my father unless I'm there with you."

"Let me correct you," Jamie said, as she tried to conceal her irritation. "He's our father. He's my father, too."

Another pause. "Look," he said. "I am his primary caregiver. I'm the one responsible for his health and wellbeing. I don't appreciate any visitors unless I'm aware of it. He gets too worked up without me around. Look what happened today; he broke Ken's nose."

Jamie smiled to herself. It was true. Ken was taller than Brett by at least an inch and thirty pounds heavier, but Brett broke his nose with the palm of his hand. "That wasn't Brett's fault. He was just protecting me."

"Let me put it this way," he said. "If you go see my father without me being there, I'll have a restraining order taken out against you. If you want to go see him, then give me a call and we'll make arrangements. Am I understood?"

"Yes," she said angrily. "But let me tell you something, Brett is my father, and I'd like to get to know him. That's all I want. I want to know who my father is."

"I've told you what you need to do. If you want to see him, make arrangements with me."

"Fine!" Jamie said angrily and disconnected the call. She sat staring out through her windshield trying to suppress her anger. Her heart was racing, and her breathing was short and quick through her nose. David had threatened her with a restraining order. His reasoning would have seemed plausible except for the fact that the only thing that appeared to agitate Brett were the townspeople.

For the entire ninety-minute drive to her mother's house from Amison, she replayed the meeting with her father through her mind. Brett had gained some lucidity. His reaction to Ken was swift, direct and controlled. He told her he had not prayed this morning. She had discovered that taking his medicine was linked to his prayer routine. That meant that he had not taken his medicine this morning. She could not help but wonder if the medicine itself was causing the problem.

She opened the camera app in her cell phone and looked at the picture she had taken of the bottle. Coznephidone. It was not surprising to her that she would not have heard of it before. She was not in the medical field. She sent a text with the picture to Curt Linden to see if he knew anything about the drug. After texting the picture, she called him.

"Hi, Jamie," he said when he answered the phone. "I just got your text. I haven't had time to look at it yet."

"Can you take a look now?"

Linden put her on speaker phone as he reviewed the picture. "OK," he said. "What's this?"

"That's the drug that Brett is taking."

"What is it?" he asked.

"I was hoping you'd have an idea."

"I've never seen this before. Is this a prescription drug?"

"It looks like it to me," she answered, "but there was no prescription tag on it. Here's the strange thing, you know how he keeps saying 'pray, pray twice a day and then pray thrice on Sunday'?"

"Yeah?"

"That's when he knows to take it. It's part of his prayer routine. He takes the drug when he prays."

"You mean it's part of his prayer ritual?" Linden asked.

"Well, yeah," Jamie answered. "Sort of. I had him show me how he prays. He kneels in front of the altar, and then he presses a couple of buttons on it that opens a hidden drawer where the drugs are kept."

"Really?" Linden asked in surprise.

"Get this," she said. "He could pretty much hold a conversation with me today. Certainly, he was a lot better than the first two times I met him. Then he told me that he did not pray this morning. That means he did not take the drug. I can't help but think they're related."

"So, what is this?" he asked contemplatively. He paused for a moment then said, "I know a pharmacist. I'll give him a call to see if he knows what it is."

"If you find out," Jamie said, "let me know, will you?"

"I will," he answered. "I'll let you go and give him a call."

~~~~

It was late afternoon when Curt Linden called with information about the drug. "Hi," he said. "I've got some info on Coznephidone."

"What do you have?" Jamie asked him.

"It's a drug that was supposed to be used for depression. It was released about seven years ago but was taken off the market about a year and a half later."

"OK," Jamie said. "So, where's he getting it?"

"I don't know. But get this: the reason it was pulled from the market is that there was a percentage of people that developed a psychosis, especially at higher dosages. The bottle Brett has is for twenty milligrams. The maximum recommended dosage per day is twenty. That means if Brett is taking the meds when he prays, then he's getting more than double the recommended dosage."

"So," Jamie said out loud as she processed the information, "his problem is happening because he's being drugged. That's got to be intentional."

"Looks that way," Linden replied. "The good news is that when the patients quit taking it, the majority of them were able to recover with little long-term effects. The psychosis reverses itself quickly. That may be why he was able to talk to you, he skipped a dose."

"Are there withdrawal symptoms?" Jamie asked.

"Minor stuff, according to what I read. Stomach cramps, diarrhea, headaches, that kind of stuff. Nothing serious."

"He's probably been on this dosage for several years."

"I would think so," Linden agreed. "The problem started just after his wife died. He was depressed then, but I didn't think he was crazy. I went to visit him to try to get him to go home and go back to work. The company needed him. I couldn't get him to leave the church. He just sat in the cemetery by Rene's grave. He grew progressively worse and then he moved into the church. David had a little apartment fixed up for him behind the front of the sanctuary. Before I had to start using this wheelchair and couldn't get in the church anymore, I saw it. It's small. Small sink and a hotplate, a tiny refrigerator, a small table and a twin sized bed. At the time all his clothes were kept in cardboard boxes. I suspect he didn't use the bed. I think he slept in the pews, but then maybe he's not sleeping at all. One of the side effects of the drug is insomnia."

"So, he's been this way since his wife died?" Jamie asked.

"Pretty much. David told me that he was seeing a local doctor. He didn't say anything about meds. That's when David took over running the business completely. David was only supposed to manage the company while his father took care of Rene. I tried to get David to have his father put in the hospital but, David refused. He said that would be like a prison for him."

"He told me the same thing."

"I'd run out and see him every couple of weeks or so, but after I started having trouble with my legs, I could only go when the weather was nice. I could always find him next to Rene's grave."

"Was he ever able to talk to you like he did to me?"

"Yes," Linden replied. "Three or four times. But even on the other days there were times when he seemed to be right there with you, only for a few seconds, and then he was gone again."

Jamie was quiet for a moment. "Can't we call the police or something?" she asked him.

"I don't think so, Jamie," Linden told her. "First of all, the whole town appears to be taking care of him. Secondly, I think David's got a sheriff's deputy in his pocket. I know for certain that he's got one checking in on him. Then I also think that someone in the health department has been paid off, too. I called the health department a few months after he moved into the church. Got a call back from someone about a day later. She told me that everything was fine, that there wasn't anything they needed to do."

"You think David did this?" Jamie asked him.

"I do," Linden said. "He was hot to take over the company at the time. He and Brett had a disagreement about taking the company public. I think Brett would have retired in just a couple of years after Rene died. But David wasn't ready to take over the company. I offered to come in and mentor him, to help him out. He really needed some more time before running a company of that size on his own. But David really didn't like me."

"I don't get it," Jamie said. "Why would someone do that to his own father?"

"David wanted that company pretty badly. When the IPO goes through, he's going to be a very wealthy man, like he isn't already very wealthy. The company makes a lot of money. Brett didn't want to go public. He seemed to think that the best way to protect the employees was to keep it private."

"So, it's all about money. That's why he drugged his father."

"That's what I think."

"So, what can we do?" Jamie asked him.

"Well, Jamie," he began. "I have to ask you; do you want to do anything at all? I mean, you don't know the man. It could be dangerous."

"Dangerous?" Jamie asked in surprise. "Why?"

"There's a lot of money at stake. If Brett really is being drugged, then there's probably going to be some jail time for someone. I think David is paying the townspeople a lot of money to be sure Brett is being taken care of. David would have been thinking that he's got everything under control but then a daughter shows up that he didn't know about. He's got to be suspicious of the timing at least. Then he's got to be wondering if you're going to make a claim on money from the IPO. I really don't know what he'd do. David isn't that smart. I wouldn't put anything past him. He can and does throw a lot of money around. If you want to step away from all this, I'll understand. I'll find another way of getting Brett some help."

Jamie was quiet as she thought about it all. "Jamie?" he asked. "Still there?"

"Yeah, I'm still here," she answered. "I'm not after anybody's money. I could have easily walked away from all this. But now I know that Brett is being drugged. That's wrong all by itself, but if there's a chance that I could actually get to know my father, then I'd like to do that. I just don't have any idea what I could do."

"I have an idea," he told her. "If we can get him off the Coznephidone, then maybe we can get him out of there. All we'd have to do is take the bottle of pills from him."

"It would just get replaced, and he'd start all over again."

"Then how about this; we replace the pills with something else, something that looks like it?"

Jamie smiled to herself. That was actually a good idea and something she could easily do. "Aspirin," she said. "The pills look a lot like regular aspirin. I'm betting that if I swapped out the pills for aspirin, Brett wouldn't know the difference and if anybody checked the bottle, they may not notice the difference either."

"Is that something you can do?" Linden asked her.

"I'll have to figure something out. The townspeople are watching for me now. They'd come running if they saw my car."

"Then don't drive your car," he told her.

"What are you thinking?" Jamie asked him.

"Rent a car that looks like David's. Get there right about sunset. It's not uncommon for David to be there about then. Do a quick run in, swap the pills and then take off. I'd bet you could be out of there before they even saw you."

"But what happens if Brett starts getting better and someone notices it?"

Linden hesitated before speaking slowly. "I don't know," he said.

"We may have to just take that chance," Jamie told him.

"I like the idea, Jamie," he told her. "Are you sure you'd want to take the risk?"

"Yeah," she answered. "I do."

Chapter 9

Jamie could hear her phone vibrating from inside her purse even though her purse was tucked into a desk drawer. She opened the drawer, pulled out her purse, retrieved her cell and checked the caller ID. It was David St. James. She answered it.

"Hello," she said.

"Hi, Jamie," David said. "Can you meet me for lunch?"

"Why?"

"I'm in town and I'd just like to talk to you for a few minutes."

"What about?" she asked him.

"I'd like to talk to you about my father. I think it would be best if we talked in person."

Jamie hesitated. She did not trust David. "OK," she said. "Where did you have in mind?"

"There's a restaurant not too far from where you work called Callub's," he said. "Can you meet me there?"

"How do you know where I work?" she asked him. She knew why he had her cell number; she gave it to him, but how did he know where she worked? The nervousness in her stomach returned.

There was a hesitation. "I can explain all that when we meet. Can we do that?"

She stiffened and clenched her teeth. She met with Curt Linden at the same restaurant. It had been a good place to meet someone. It was public and some of the waitresses knew her by name. "OK," she said. "What time?"

"Twelve thirty?"

"Sure," she answered. Then, as an afterthought, she added, "I'm bringing someone with me."

"Who?"

"I don't know you, David," she said. "Caution tells me not to meet a man I don't know like this all by myself."

Another hesitation. "OK," he said. "Twelve thirty at Callub's"

~~~

Phil held the door for Jamie, letting her walk into the restaurant ahead of him. She walked in with a surge of confidence as Phil followed closely behind her. He projected an air that said he was taking his job as Jamie's protector seriously. He stood tall and strong. His jaw was clenched and jutted out. His eyes were alert and attentive.

Jamie spotted David looking at them from a booth next to the windows. Without smiling, he acknowledged her with a nod. Jamie pointed David out to Phil and they joined him at the booth. David held his hand out to Jamie to shake it as she slid into the booth across from him. Jamie shook it. David then shook Phil's hand as he sat on the outside edge of the bench. "I'm David St. James," David said to him.

"Phil," he replied without giving his last name.

"Thanks for coming," David said to Jamie as the waitress placed glasses of water in front of them. They were each handed a menu. Jamie and Phil both laid them flat on the table without opening them.

"So, what did you need to see me about?" Jamie asked him.

David laid his menu on the table and looked her squarely in the eyes. "Jamie," he began. "I didn't know that I had a half-sister before I met you. Even after Dad told us we were brother and sister I didn't believe it, so I had you checked out. I had someone do a background check on you."

"Let me guess," Jamie said, "a private investigator."

"Sort of," David said. "She's just someone that specialized on background checks. That's how I knew where you worked."

"And that wasn't something you could tell me over the phone?" Jamie asked.

David took in a deep breath and let it out again. He looked at her in a way that suggested to Jamie he was trying to keep his impatience in check. Only a flicker in his eyes betrayed what he was feeling. "That's right," he said. "There's just some conversations that should take place in person."

"OK," Jamie said, "what else did you find out about me?"

"Well," he said, "it took a while, but I found out how we are related. Do you know the story?"

"I know one version of the story," she said. "What's yours?"

"Here's what I found out; my father and your mother had an affair. I think I might have been seven at the time. He broke it off with your mother before you were born."

"He broke it off?" Jamie asked.

"Yes. But your mother was making it difficult for my father and blackmailed him."

"What?" Jamie asked incredulously. "That didn't happen."

"I know someone who was there. He told me the whole story," he said as he tilted his head up.

Jamie glanced at Phil, who was staring at David through narrowing eyes. David remained focused on Jamie. She turned back to face him and glared back angrily. "I know someone who was there, too; my mother! That did not happen."

"In any case," David continued. "I need you to keep away from him. I understand why you might want to get to know who your biological father is, especially since he's wealthy, but in his condition, you really can't have any type of relationship with him. He's not going to get better. His dementia is only going to grow worse until I'm forced to put him in a home. No rational person would ever think that they could have a genuine relationship with him. Just the fact that you've shown up has thrown him off his routine. With his issues, he needs routine."

"I'm not so sure he'll never recover," Jamie told him.

"So, now you have a medical degree," David said sarcastically.

"I had a decent conversation with him the other day," Jamie told him. "You can't tell me he can't get better. He knows who I am."

"He knows your name," David said impatiently. "That's pretty much it."

"He knows I'm his daughter! You can't tell me that someone who can make carvings like he can, is never going to be able to have any relationships at all. You just can't. He's still in there and I'm going to prove it." Jamie flinched internally. Had she said too much? She did not want to let slip that she was aware that it was the medication causing the problem and that he would probably recover once he was off it.

David narrowed his eyes at her. "What do you mean?" he asked.

Jamie quickly came up with a plausible explanation of what she meant. "I mean, that if I can spend a little time with him, have normal conversations with him, I think he'll start to get better."

David sat back hard in his seat and angrily pushed his menu across the table at Jamie. It slid under her menu and stopped. She flinched backwards with a gasp.

"Hey!" Phil said loudly at David. David turned to face him and the two men locked eyes, exchanging angry glares. A moment passed. Without breaking the stare, Phil reached over and took the two menus from in front of Jamie, stacked them with his own and dropped all three on the floor beside him.

David looked away first, turning back to Jamie. "The timing of all this is suspicious, you showing up at just this time."

"I only showed up because I received a letter asking me to."

"Fine. OK," David said. "Now, what will it take for you not to show up again?" Jamie began to speak but David interrupted her. "I'd like you to just go away." David interrupted again as Jamie began to speak. "How much will it take for you to just disappear?"

"I'm not asking anything from you," Jamie said angrily.

"Will a hundred K do it?" David sneered.

"What?" Jamie demanded.

David raised his voice. "How much will it take to make you go away like your whore of a mother did?"

Jamie was stunned to silence. Her eyes widened, and her mouth hung open. She held her breath as her face turned crimson. Phil tensed his body. He leaned forward. Curling his fingers into a claw he raised his hands inches off the table, preparing to reach over and grab David by the shirt. David clenched his teeth so hard that the muscles in his jaw bulged. He raised both hands off the table between himself and Phil, one in a fist and the other open, fingers splayed wide apart. His eyebrows pinched together, and he took a noisy, deep breath through his nose

Jamie placed her hand on Phil's shoulder. "We're leaving," she told him while looking at David. She gave Phil a gentle push to signal him to let her out of the booth. Phil visibly released some of the building tension and stood at the end of the booth glaring down at David. He held out his hand to assist Jamie out.

Jamie turned to face David. Her face was turning a darker crimson. David looked up at her. He raised one side of his upper lip in a scowl at her. He clenched both hands into fists and placed them knuckles down on the table. Jamie stared angrily at him for a moment. She leaned over, put the back of her hand on Phil's water glass and flung it across the table. David flinched backwards as the glass hit him in the chest and fell to his lap. He scrambled to brush the water off before it had a chance to soak into his suit. Jamie turned and began walking quickly towards the door with Phil following closely behind.

David yelled after her. "If you go near him again, I'll take out a Personal Protection Order against you."

Jamie slowed her pace for a moment. Phil turned to look at David over his shoulder. Jamie resumed her pace and left the restaurant.

~~~~~~

Jamie and Phil returned to the office. Phil followed her to her cube where she sat heavily into her chair. "You OK?" he asked.

"I'm fine," she answered.

"What are you going to do?"

"I don't know. I'll need some time to think about it. I'm just too angry right now."

"Well, OK," Phil told her. "But if you need me, let me know. I may be able to help."

Jamie looked at him from her chair, smiled and nodded. "Thanks, Phil," she said. "Thanks for coming with me but I shouldn't have dragged you into this."

"That's fine," he said. "It gave me a bit of excitement for the day. But please, don't go near him again, at least not without someone being there with you. There's something about him that's kind of creepy, if you ask me."

"Can you believe that is the guy in charge of Tashe International?" she asked him.

"Really," Phil asked in surprise. "You didn't tell me that."

"He's the CEO."

"Wow," Phil said. "That's hard to believe."

"It's true. My father owns it and David is running it."

"Makes you wonder what would have happened if you would have actually known your father when you grew up. Maybe you'd be the CEO," Phil commented.

Jamie huffed. "Doubt it. I wouldn't have the first clue about running something like that."

"Well, OK," Phil said. "I need to get back to my desk. You let me know if I can help you in some way. If you want me to go with you to see your father again, let me know."

"I will," Jamie replied. "Thank you."

Phil left Jamie sitting in her chair several inches from her desk. She rolled her chair closer and put her purse in the desk drawer. She stared at the dark screen of her computer. Her hands were trembling. Her entire body seemed to shake, and her stomach twisted in knots. She closed her eyes and focused on her breathing, trying to relax, but visions of David sneering at her kept breaking her focus. She gave up, retrieved a cup of coffee from the kitchen and sat down at a table in the lunchroom. She stared into her coffee.

Minutes passed before she had calmed herself enough to return to her desk. She freshened her coffee and walked slowly. What David had told her echoed through her mind. Had her mother blackmailed Brett St. James? Perhaps that was the real reason that she kept him a secret from her so long. She did not think that was something her mother would do but that would have happened before she was born. The thought haunted her.

She sat at her desk and again stared at the blank computer screen for several moments. Her mind raced to review her options. She could ignore David's demands and go see her father without him. She could ask David to be there when she went to see Brett, or she could simply forget all about Brett and David St. James and move on with her life. She was beginning to believe that forgetting all about them and moving on was her best option.

Her computer screen came to life when she touched the mouse and she unlocked it with her password. What was she doing before she broke for lunch? Why was David being such a jerk? Did her mother blackmail Brett St. James? What difference would it make if she got to know her father? Was any of this worth her time? Brett was the father she had always wanted to know. He may not have been the father that she had always dreamed of, but he was still her father. But then again, he was just her biological father. That did not make him a real father. Real fathers know their kids, love them, teach them and take care of them. They had relationships with their children. Was it too late now to have a relationship with him? What if David was right and Brett did have Alzheimer's? What if she went through all this effort to get to know a man who obviously did not want to know her while she was growing up and then found out he still did not care or want to know anything about her? If he was in his right mind would he still be interested in her?

But wait. Brett never said he wanted to know her. That was Curt Linden who told her that. He's the one who led her to her biological father. If Brett had wanted to know her why did he not do it when he was not on the drug and had the ability to reason? Perhaps he really did not want to know her. But then again, all those carvings of her, what did they mean? He obviously had seen her at least a few times. Was it only because he did not want his wife to know about the affair? Or was there something more? Perhaps he felt that she was just a mistake, something to sweep under the rug. Wasn't that what she actually was? Wasn't that what he actually did? Perhaps her mother did blackmail him. Perhaps none of this mattered and she should just move on with her life, let this all simply fade away like a bad memory she wished she did not have.

Half-brother. David. Shoot. Her attention shifted to a more immediate focus. She needed to call Curt Linden and tell him what happened with David.

She pulled out her cell phone and dialed him from her contacts list.

"Curt Linden," he said when he answered it.

"Hi, Curt," she said. "It's Jamie."

"Hi Jamie. What's up?"

"I met with David today for lunch," she told him.

"Why?" Linden asked.

"He called me and wanted to meet. So, we met at the same restaurant you and I met at."

"What did he want?"

"He told me to stay away from Brett. He even offered to give me money to stay away from him."

"How much?" Linden asked.

"A hundred thousand dollars," she answered.

"What did you say?"

"I didn't say anything. I just left."

"That's good, Jamie," Linden said. "The less you say to him the better."

"He called my mother a whore," Jamie told him. "He said that my mother blackmailed Brett."

"That didn't happen, Jamie." Linden sounded surprised. "I know that didn't happen. As a matter of fact, Carol Ann tried to refuse the money he offered her. Brett insisted."

"That's good to know. He said he heard it from someone that was there. Any idea who that might be?"

Linden paused to think about it. "No. I have no idea. As far as I know it was only me who knew about it. Even Brett said I was the only one who knew."

"That would mean that David is lying then," Jamie said.

"I wouldn't put it past him. He's been known to embellish the truth a bit."

"I'm not sure what to do now," she told him. "I'm thinking it may not be worth my effort. David said if I went back he'd take out a Personal Protection Order against me."

Linden chuckled in the phone. "That doesn't mean anything. If you were to get Brett off that medicine, then Brett could simply order it rescinded."

"Yeah," she said, "but how can I do that if I can't see him?"

"I told you before how to do that," Linden told her. "Rent a car that looks like David's then show up at sundown. The townspeople will think it's David visiting Brett and will leave you alone."

Jamie considered it for a moment. "I don't know, Curt," she told him. "A doctor is prescribing his meds. If I take him off it, will it do more harm than good?"

"Jamie, Coznephidone is a bad drug. It's been off the market for at least five years. He's taking over double the maximum dosage. If you take him off it, you'll be saving his life. All you need to do is swap that drug out for some aspirin. Then go back in a couple of days. He'll be grateful that you did. And let's be honest, you don't know that an actual doctor is prescribing that drug."

Jamie hesitated.

"You'll be saving his life, Jamie," Linden repeated.

"OK, OK," Jamie said. "Let me think about it."

"I know you'll do the right thing, Jamie."

Ralph Nelson Willett

Chapter 10

Jamie felt small sitting behind the wheel of such a large vehicle. The Cadillac Escalade was much larger than anything she had driven before. Curt Linden had taken the time to locate a car rental for her that could rent a white Escalade. From what she remembered of David's SUV it was a near perfect match. Anyone who was not up close to it would believe it was David's car parked in front of the church.

She planned her drive to Amison to arrive at the church at dusk. That would let the townspeople see the car well enough to think that it was David parked out front. She would take an indirect route, so she would not have to pass through the town. This would make it less likely that someone would see it was her driving the car and not David. She wanted to be as invisible as possible, so she took some time to look at the owner's manual to try and understand how to turn off the headlights before she started out. She turned them off almost a mile outside of Amison.

She parked the Escalade facing downtown in front of the church. She did not see anyone, but she waited a couple of minutes, watching to see if anyone had noticed her, before going in.

It was dark inside the church. The only light in the sanctuary was from four large candles standing on the altar. She called out for Brett. There was no answer. Moving quickly, she went to the altar, pressed the heads of the two cherubs and popped open the little drawer. She pulled out the bottle of Coznephidone and dumped out its contents on top of the altar. She retrieved a bottle of generic aspirin from her purse and shook out enough on the altar to create a small pile of pills about the same size as the pile of the prescription drug. The two drugs looked very similar. The only difference she could see was that the real drug had intersecting lines going down the middle of it along with the number twenty-nine etched on its side.

She held the bottle of Coznephidone against the edge of the altar and using the palm of her hand she slid the aspirin into it. She put the bottle back in the drawer and snapped it shut. The real prescription pills she brushed into a plastic bag, zipped it closed, and put it in her purse.

She shouted out Brett's name, again. No response. She looked around and saw that there was light bleeding out from under the door that led to the basement area. Moving as quickly as possible she went through the door and down the stairs.

The lower level was brightly lit. She heard the same tapping she had heard the first time she had come down here. It was the sound of Brett working on another carving in the back room. She noticed that most of the carvings that were on the table were missing. Perhaps only a third of what was there before remained. A closer look at the carvings revealed that the missing ones were all the carvings of her. No time to consider why, she moved quickly to the back room where she found Brett with a hammer and chisel in hand. "Hi, Brett," she said more calmly than her adrenalin demanded of her.

Brett turned to face her with a snap of his head. He grinned happily at her. "Jamie, Jamie, Jamie, Jamie, Jamie," he repeated, as he gently set his tools down on the workbench. "Jamie, Jamie, Jamie, pray, pray twice a day and then pray thrice on Sunday." He sang the words. His face lit up with excitement as if he suddenly remembered something important. He held up a finger to indicate he wanted her to wait. He slid past her quickly through the door into the common area.

"Brett," Jamie said as he brushed by. "I have to hurry. I need to tell you something."

Brett hurried to the center of the room and stopped abruptly, his back to her. He turned slowly as he looked at the near empty tables on either side of him and then turned to face Jamie as she stood in the doorway of the workshop.

"Brett?" Jamie inquired.

Brett's face turned gloomy with deep disappointment in his eyes. He faced the tables to his left and swept his arm in front of him slowly. "Jamie, Jamie, Jamie," he said sadly.

"They're gone, Brett," she told him gently. "I don't know where they went."

He turned and faced her, hung his arms by his side with slumped shoulders. He hung his head.

"Brett, I'm sorry," Jamie told him as she slowly walked to him. She put her hand on his shoulder and squeezed it gently. "I'm sorry. I don't know what happened."

Brett looked into her face as his eyes began to tear.

"It's OK, Brett," she told him. "You can make more. It's OK."

He hung his head again. "Jamie," he whispered.

Jamie took one of his hands and held it with both of hers. "Brett, I need to tell you something. You need to give me all of your attention. Please. I need to hurry."

Brett looked into her eyes. It was a moment when Jamie felt as if he was really with her, that his mind was clear enough to hear what she had to tell him.

"Brett," she said. "I've switched out your medicine. It's just aspirin. It looks just like the drug you were taking. I need you to take the aspirin just like you took the other medicine. Pray, pray, twice a day and then pray thrice on Sunday. Can you do that?"

Brett showed no reaction. He held her eyes with his.

"Brett, someone has given you a bad drug. It has side effects that can make you look like you're crazy. I know you're not crazy, Brett. We can make you better. Do you understand?"

No reaction. His eyes seemed to fade away even as he looked at her. Nothing indicated that he heard her.

Jamie pressed on hoping that somehow, she was getting through. "And this is important," she continued. "If someone comes to see you, you must continue to act as if you were still on the drug. They can't know that you're not taking it anymore. If they think you're not taking the drug, then they'll make you take it again and then you can't get better."

Brett stood still and quiet. His face was expressionless, and he looked away from her to the near-empty tables again.

"Brett," Jamie said. "Please, I need you to give me a sign that you understand."

Brett swept his arm over the row of tables again.

"Brett," Jamie said. "Did you understand me?"

He faced her directly again, tears still welling in his eyes. "Jamie, Jamie, Jamie," he said quietly. "Pray, pray twice a day." He slumped his shoulders and hung his head again.

Jamie reached in and wrapped her arms around him, hugging him tightly. "Please, Brett. Please understand me," Jamie said above a whisper. Brett returned her hug gently. She held him for a moment and then stepped back. "I'm sorry, Brett. I have to go. If they catch me here, I'll be in trouble. I'll come back in a couple of days. I promise." She paused a moment and then rushed back to the stairway leading upstairs to the sanctuary. She hurried through the vestibule and out of the front door.

She moved quickly down the steps and jogged back to the Escalade. She opened the door and stood behind it looking through the window towards town. It was almost completely dark. In the dim light she saw two people moving quickly towards her about a block's distance away. She quickly climbed in, started the car and made a U-turn in the middle of the street. The big SUV ran up on the grass on the opposite side of the road. As soon as she completed the turn, she sped off, quickly leaving the town behind her. Looking in the rearview mirror she saw that the two people were now standing in the middle of the road watching her drive away.

Chapter 11

Jamie was unfamiliar with the older woman waiting patiently in the office lobby. She smiled up at Jamie as Jamie came out of the office area to greet her. When the receptionist had called to let her know she had a visitor, she had not been expecting anyone. The visit came as a surprise. The woman had to have been in her late sixties, perhaps early seventies. She wore a blue patterned dress that was buttoned up to her neck and black orthopedic shoes. She reminded Jamie of a stereotypical grandmother.

"Can I help you?" she asked the woman.

The woman slid forward to the edge of her chair in short scoots and stiffly stood. She winced as she straightened and took a moment to take a couple of breaths. "Are you Jamie Fulton?" the woman asked, as she forced a smile.

"Yes," Jamie replied.

The woman slid her large purse around from her side to the front of her. She opened it with a slow, deliberate movement and pulled out an envelope. She held it out to Jamie with a tremoring hand. Jamie looked at the envelope being held out to her and reflexively took it. "You've been served," the woman said, as she closed her purse with the same slow, deliberate movements she had opened it with. The woman turned and with a quick ambling walk that looked painful, left the reception area, and left the building.

Jamie was stunned. She opened the envelope and read its contents. A Personal Protection Order had been taken out against her. She had been ordered to remain at least one thousand feet from Brett St. James.

Her chest and stomach tightened. The blood rushed to her face as she clenched her teeth. Her neck muscles tightened to the point that her head shook.

David must have found out that she had visited Brett two days before. She had hoped that she would not have been recognized, but she obviously was. How? It was dark enough that no one should have known it was her. What gave her away?

She moved quickly back to her cube and reread the document more carefully. She pulled her cell phone from her purse and called David. His phone rang several times. Her thoughts shifted to the angry message she was going to leave in his voicemail when he answered the call.

"Hello, Jamie," David said calmly through the phone.

Her thoughts shifted again. "What is this?" Jamie asked, nearly shouting into the phone.

The Legacy

"So, you've been served, I see. It's a PPO," he said. "I warned you not to go near my father."

"You didn't have to do this!"

"Apparently, I did. I told you that if you went near him again, I would do this. You obviously didn't believe me. I do what I say I'm going to do. If you go back, I'll have you arrested."

"He's my father, too!" Jamie shouted at him as she stood from her chair. She shook the PPO in front of her as if David could see it. "This says that I threatened him!"

"You're nothing more than a mistake," he shouted back angrily at her. "You mean nothing to him!"

"You're an idiot if that's what you believe. You saw all those carvings of me! There's no way you can say that I don't mean something to him!" Jamie was breathing heavily, her eyes roiled in anger as she stared straight ahead.

There was a pause before David calmly and quietly asked, "What carvings?"

David had the carvings removed. The realization hit Jamie like a slap in the face. He intentionally removed anything that might be evidence that his father wished to have a connection with her. She lowered her voice to match his and slowly said, "You," she paused, "are evil."

"Whatever, Jamie," he responded coldly. "But listen. Don't go anywhere near my father again and never call me again. It's over. Understand?"

Jamie had an idea and spoke it out in a frustrated desperation. She calmly said, "I wonder what the business press would have to say about any of this. It might make an interesting story. I mean, where has the owner of Tashe International been these last few years? People just might be interested in that, especially investors."

Jamie could tell by David's voice that he was speaking through clenched teeth. She could almost feel him trying to contain his anger. "If anything at all appears in the press, about him, me, my company, anything at all, then I will make your life a living hell." Jamie started to say something, but David interrupted her. "And your mother's!" he added loudly. "You know I can and I promise you, I will."

~~~~

Jamie hung up the phone. She was shaken. She had no doubt that if she went to the press David would make good on his threat. She had no doubt that with his money he could be creatively vindictive. That was not something that she wanted to go through and she certainly did not want her mother dragged into it.

Her supervisor stepped into her cube. "What's going on?" she asked.

Jamie was breathing heavily and staring angrily down at her keyboard. She took a deep breath and forced herself to relax.

"Are you OK?" her supervisor asked.

Jamie's face burned with anger. She held up the court document for her boss to take. She took it, unfolded it and looked it over briefly. "What's this?" she asked Jamie.

"I've just been served with a PPO," Jamie told her as she tried to suppress her anger even further.

"Who is Brett St. James?" she asked Jamie.

"My biological father."

Her supervisor looked at the document more closely. "It says you threatened him. Did you?"

Jamie slammed the palms of her hands down on her desktop. "No, I didn't threaten him!" Jamie shouted.

"Calm down," she told Jamie. "Why don't you take a break for a while."

Jamie stared at her angrily. She flexed her leg hard backwards, pushing the chair back. It banged against the two-drawer filing cabinet by her desk. She glared angrily at her boss.

"Jamie," her supervisor said, speaking more forcefully. "Take a break." Jamie began to walk past her. "If you need to talk, you can come see me," she told Jamie. Jamie stopped and looked at her with fire in her eyes. She paused a moment, pursed her lips together and nodded curtly before walking away.

Jamie left the building and walked the sidewalk at an angry pace. Her office was in the center of a large campus with several buildings surrounded by parking lots. It covered three-square blocks. She walked around the outside edge of the buildings twice before she had calmed herself down enough to think coherently. She crossed her arms and stared down at the sidewalk as her pace slowed.

David did warn her that if she went to see her father without him, he would file a restraining order. She tried to be careful, to not be seen, but still she had been recognized. How? The PPO said that she had threatened Brett. In what way had she appeared threatening? There was nothing she did or said that could have been misconstrued as threatening. At least not to Brett. Maybe to David. If David found out she knew what he was doing to his father, that could be threatening. But the PPO said that *she* had threatened Brett. Since she never threatened him, that meant that David had lied to the court.

Her anger spiked again. An angry shiver passed through her body. Again, she fought to control her emotions.

Now, she had a problem she needed to deal with. She had swapped out Brett's medicine for aspirin. She had planned on returning tonight to check on him, to see if he was alright, to see if it had made a difference. Now, everyone would be watching for her and she would be arrested if she showed up in town. Even the restaurant would have been within the one-thousand-foot exclusion zone the court put around Brett. Did she want to risk going to jail or should she simply let it all go? She was happier when she did not know who her father was. Why did she have to know now? He was not her problem. She could easily wash her hands of the entire mess.

She considered the PPO. Now, that one had been taken out against her, should she contact a lawyer? She did not have one. She never needed one before. How much would that cost? Would it be worth it if it meant she could get to know her father? Her next call should be to Curt Linden. She would make that call from home tonight.

Jamie's return to her cube took her past her supervisor's office. She stopped Jamie and called her back. "You OK?" she asked.

Jamie stopped and stood apprehensively in the doorway. "Yeah," she told her. "I'm fine. Sorry about my outburst."

"I didn't know you found out who your father was," her boss said.

"I found out just a few weeks ago. His name is Brett St. James."

Her boss looked down for a moment. "That name sounds familiar."

"He owns Tashe International," Jamie told her.

Her boss's eyes widened, and she tilted her head in surprise. "Your father owns Tashe?"

"My biological father," Jamie corrected. "His son is running it now. Brett's actually gone nuts. He's lost his mind. He can't even talk to you normally."

"Oh. That's too bad. Sorry to hear that. Alzheimer's?"

"I don't think so. I think it might be a reaction to a drug he's taking. I went to see him the other night to try to find out. That's what the PPO is all about. They don't want me near him."

"So, what are you going to do?"

"I don't know. Maybe I'm better off not knowing who my father is. What difference would it make anyhow?"

"You may be right," her supervisor said calmly.

Jamie was silent for a moment and then stepped back from the doorway. "Well, I better get back to my desk. Sorry about what happened."

"Well, if you need to talk some more, come see me, OK?"

"I will," Jamie replied. "Thank you."

~~~~

It was eight thirty before Jamie worked up the courage to call Curt Linden. She toyed with her cell phone with one hand and petted Sheba, who purred quietly in her lap, with her other. It was time to tell Linden she was through with all this. She forced herself to make the call.

"Hi, Jamie," Linden said as he answered the phone.

"Hi," Jamie replied.

"How's your father?"

"I don't know. That's part of why I'm calling."

"What's going on?" Linden asked.

"David served me with a PPO this morning."

"Oh?" Linden said with a bit of surprise in his voice. "The jerk actually did it. I didn't think he would."

"I told him I'd go to the press. He said if I did, he'd make my life and my mother's a living hell." Jamie paused, then added, "I think he would, too."

"Yeah," Linden said. "Don't go to the press. That's a bad idea. You don't know what David will do. There's no reason to bring all that grief down on you."

"I know," Jamie replied.

"So, what are you going to do?"

"That's why I'm calling," Jamie said. "There really isn't anything I can do. I don't want to be arrested. I think I'd just like to let it all go. There really isn't anything in this for me."

"What do you mean there isn't anything in this for you? Did you swap out the medicine?"

"Yeah. Two nights ago."

"Well," Linden said, "if he gets better, then you actually may be able to get to know your father. I'd say that would be something for you."

"I know," Jamie replied. "But I don't have a way to know if swapping out his medicine for aspirin did anything for him. He might be worse as far as I know."

"Jamie, we know what that drug does. We know he's getting a larger dosage than the maximum dosage allowed. I think it's a question we'd both like an answer to; did he get better after you took him off it?"

"I'm not supposed to be within a thousand feet of him," Jamie told him.

"Jamie, don't you understand how a PPO works?" Linden said. "The first time they catch you with him it isn't a big deal. You claim ignorance or play dumb or something. The cops will just give you a stern warning and then let you go. Think about it. You're a petite woman, who weighs what, 100, 110 pounds? He's a big man that is probably more than twice your weight. No cop in his right mind would think that you're there to hurt him. You couldn't possibly hurt him. They won't want to take you to jail. This isn't a problem."

"Are you sure?" Jamie asked him.

"My son was a cop in Michigan before he retired. I know how this works. Call it insider information if you will."

"I don't know..."

"Jamie," he interrupted, "here's what I suggest you do. Go back in that rented Escalade again. About the same time or maybe a little later to let it get darker. Then just go and see if Brett is any better. If not, you leave, and you're done.

You'll know the answer right away if taking him off the medicine worked or not."

"What if he *is* better?" she asked him.

"Then leave and take him with you. Go straight to the hospital and explain what happened. They'll get the necessary people involved."

"Don't you think David will come after me?"

"He might try," Linden said. "But I know Brett. Once he's in his right mind, he'll want to take care of all this. Not only that, he'll be thrilled to finally get to know his daughter in person rather than having to watch her from a distance."

"You're sure about going to jail?" Jamie asked hesitantly.

"No jail," Linden laughed.

"Alright," Jamie said. "I'll think about it."

Linden became serious again. "Jamie, you'll be saving his life. I know you'll do the right thing."

Ralph Nelson Willett

Chapter 12

"Why would you trust this guy?" Phil asked Jamie as his eyes narrowed. "What he's telling you isn't true. If you've been served with a PPO and you violate it, you're going to jail." Sitting across from one another at the only table in the small break room, they chatted over coffee. Jamie was telling Phil about her last conversation with Linden.

"His son was a cop. I think he knows what he's talking about." She held her coffee cup with two hands, resting them on the table. Phil kept his eyes focused on her as he sat across from her. Jamie's eyes darted around the room, avoiding eye contact.

"It doesn't matter if his son was a cop or not," Phil insisted. "Maybe where his son was a cop, it's different but around here, violating a PPO will get you arrested."

"You see," she said finally making eye contact. "That just doesn't make sense to me. I think he's right. The first time you violate a PPO, you can plead ignorance and promise not to do it again. They give you a firm warning and send you on your way."

"Jamie," Phil said, "please don't do this. You've been told to stay away. You're smarter than that. What reason do you have to believe anything he says?"

"I have to know if it was the drug that was making him that way. If it was, then he'll be better. If not, then no harm done. I never have to go back. But I *have* to know."

There was an awkward moment of silence broken by Phil. "From what you've told me about the old man in the wheelchair, I can't help but feel like something isn't right. If you went to jail, would he bail you out? What about the cost of the lawyer? Can you afford that?"

"I won't be arrested," Jamie insisted. "I'll be in and out before anyone knows that I was even there."

"Please, Jamie. Don't go. Let the old man go. It's still nice weather so he can meet with him outside."

Jamie puffed her cheeks out and blew out a long breath as she looked out of the breakroom window. The conversation was not going as she had hoped it would. She was not sure what she expected Phil to say, but he certainly was not being supportive.

She nodded her head slowly. "OK," she told him. "I'll get him to go."

"Thank you," he said. He reached his hand out across the table to her. She looked at his hand blankly for a moment before she reached out and took it with hers. She gave him a weak smile.

"I don't want anything to happen to you," Phil told her. "There's just something about all this that doesn't feel right to me." He gave her hand a gentle squeeze and then released it.

~~~

"Jamie, I can't," Linden said through the cell phone. His voice carried a sense of dismay that she would even ask him such a thing. "My legs are giving me a lot of pain. I'm on some heavy pain killers now so I don't dare drive anywhere."

Jamie's mind raced. She had asked him to go to the church and check on Brett. His inability to make the trip to Amison was making things difficult. "Maybe I can drive you there," she told him.

There was silence on the line for a moment. "Even if you did drive me, you couldn't get me close enough without being within the exclusion zone. Then, if you're that close, you might as well run in and see for yourself. You'd be in and out within 90 seconds. You'd know right away if taking Brett off the Coznephidone brought back the man we both love or not."

Jamie rested her elbow on her desk, placed her forehead in the palm of her hand and held her cell phone to her ear with her other hand. She closed her eyes and tried to reason through what she should do next.

"Jamie?" Linden prompted.

"Are you sure about just getting a warning the first time?"

"Yes. I'm sure."

"Let me think about it, OK?" Her voice was soft and timid.

Linden softened his voice to match hers. "I know you're afraid of being arrested. I understand. But you have to trust me on this."

"If I'm arrested will you come and bail me out?"

Linden chucked. "Sure. I'll do that."

"OK," Jamie said quietly.

"Jamie, I know I've told you this before, but you may be saving his life."

"I know."

"So, you'll do it?"

"We'll see," she said. "What if I just called David and told him I wanted to see Brett for a few minutes? If he comes with me, there wouldn't be a problem."

"You can't. He's the one giving him the drugs. And why would he let you go with him when he just took out a PPO against you?"

Jamie closed her eyes as she rested her head in her palm. She really needed to know if taking Brett off the Coznephidone worked or not. She had to find out before David did. Maybe before even Doc did or any of the other townspeople. If a doctor was helping David, and taking Brett off the drug worked, then it would not be long before they found out and forced him back on the drug.

"OK," Jamie finally said. "I'll head out there after work. If I time it right, I can be there around seven or seven thirty. I can be in and out in just a few seconds. Hopefully no one will see me so there won't be a problem."

"There won't be a problem, Jamie," Linden said. "If there is, you call me, and we'll work it out."

"OK," she said. "I'll call you as soon as I know something."

~~~

Jamie approached the church from the far side of town to avoid driving through it. Her stomach turned in knots to the point she wanted to vomit. Her hands were shaking and even with the car's air conditioning turned all the way up, she still had beads of sweat forming on her forehead. She wished she could have told Phil where she was going, but she already knew what his reaction would have been.

She stopped the car outside of town, close enough that she could see the church. There were no cars parked in front of the church. She watched to see if she could see anyone walking around town. The town was quiet. There was no one she could see.

She took several quick breaths and pressed down hard on the accelerator. The Toyota raced toward the church. As she approached the front of the church, she stepped on the brakes. She had misjudged her speed and pressed the brakes harder. She turned her wheels towards the shoulder of the road and as the tires touched the gravel the antilock brakes engaged. The brake pedal vibrated hard and pushed back against her foot. She pushed harder. A cloud of dust kicked up all around her. The car rolled several feet beyond where she wanted to stop. When the car finally came to a rest, she quickly put it in reverse and backed up until she was behind the sidewalk leading to the church.

She pulled her keys out, opened the door and was about to make a quick dash for the front door when she saw the sheriff's deputy car race into view from the restaurant parking lot. All its lights were flashing, including the headlights which rapidly flashed alternately, first one side and then the other. The car raced directly at her and stopped at an angle in front of her car, kicking up another cloud of dust as its front tires hit the gravel.

Jamie's hand had been on the car door, about to close it when the deputy's car raced toward her. She froze in place. Her eyes were wide, and she held her breath. The deputy quickly exited the car, drew his pistol and pointed it at her over the hood of his car.

"Get on the ground!" he yelled at her. "Get on the ground!" Jamie raised both hands and began dropping to her knees. "Get on the ground!" he yelled again.

"Ok," Jamie said loudly. "I am! I am!" She dropped fully to her knees, placed her hands on the gravel in front of her and began to lower herself to her stomach.

"I said get on the ground!"

"I am! I'm down! I'm down!" she yelled, as she lay flat on the gravel.

Jamie was unsure of what to do with her hands. Should she stretch them out in front of her or put them on top of her head? She quickly decided to put them on top of her head like she had seen people do on TV shows.

"Hand's on your head!" the deputy yelled at her as he moved quickly around the front of his car towards her.

"They are!" Jamie yelled back. She turned her head to the side to try to keep her face out of the gravel. It dug into the side of her cheek.

The deputy holstered his weapon and placed a heavy knee in the middle of her back. It pushed the air out of Jamie's lungs. She let out a loud "uhhhh" with the pressure.

"Stop resisting!" the cop yelled, as he took her left hand and moved it behind her back and placed a handcuff on it.

"I'm not!" Jamie offered no resistance and let the deputy pull her arms around behind her.

He cuffed her wrists together. "Stop resisting!" the cop shouted, as he turned her over on her backside. He roughly sat her up straight. Jamie's shoulders slumped, and she hung her head. Her hair fell on both sides of her face like curtains.

His hand grabbed a handful of her hair and pulled hard to tilt her head back. "I said stop resisting!" he shouted. He held something in front of her face. She realized what it was microseconds before the pepper spray caught her full in the eyes. She screamed in pain as her eyes involuntarily slammed shut. She inhaled a lungful as she gasped for air. She choked on the pepper spray as she inhaled more with each scream. She rolled to her side in the gravel and writhed. Taking short breaths, she coughed with each one. Curling into a ball and moaning in pain, she desperately tried to turn her head enough to wipe her eyes with the shoulder of her blouse but could not reach it. Tears gushed as her eyes tried to flush the pepper away. She coughed violently for several seconds. When her body became accustomed to the pain, all she could do was whimper "why?"

Chapter 13

Phil was by Jamie's side as they walked to his car, parked in the Sheriff's parking lot. Her pace was slow. Her shoulders slumped. She hung her head and kept her bloodshot eyes cast down. Phil glanced over at her, walked a few paces and glanced again. Neither spoke a word. He opened his car door for her. She climbed in, placed her hands on her lap and stared at her feet. Phil closed the door gently behind her, walked around to the driver's side, climbed in and sat behind the wheel. He put his keys in the ignition but did not start the car. "Are you OK?" he asked her.

Jamie did not respond. Phil nodded and turned the ignition key. He put his hand on the gear shift just as Jamie spoke. "I was arrested," she said quietly.

"I'm sorry," he responded quietly in return.

She lifted teary eyes towards him. "Do you have any idea what that's like?"

"No," he said gently.

She wiped her eyes and returned to staring at her feet. "They pepper sprayed me for no reason."

"I know. I'm sorry. Is there anything I can do for you, Jamie?"

"No," she answered weakly.

Phil put his foot on the brake, shifted the car into reverse and looked over his shoulder to begin pulling out of the parking space. "Phil?" Jamie prompted without looking up. He glanced back at her. "Thank you for bailing me out." She had tried to call Linden, but he did not answer his phone.

"You're welcome. I'm glad I could help."

"I really don't know what I would have done without you. I couldn't call my mother."

"I'm glad I could be there for you."

She leaned her head against the passenger door window. "It was like they were waiting for me," she said, more to herself than to Phil. "He sprayed pepper spray in my eyes."

"I'll take you home. It looks like you haven't slept all night."

"I didn't."

Phil began backing out of the parking space. "I have to get my car," she told him.

He pulled out of the space, put the car in drive and straightened the car out. He stopped and turned to focus his full attention on Jamie. "Jamie," he began. "I think it's going to be best if we let your car sit in the impound lot for tonight. You're in no shape to drive the hour and a half home. I'll take you home, so you can get some rest. Then I can bring you back to the impound lot tomorrow. Your car will be fine where it is for now."

She closed her eyes. "OK," she said just above a whisper.

The ride was quiet until they reached the interstate. "Phil?" Jamie said quietly.

"Yeah?" he answered in the same quiet voice.

"I'm sorry."

"For what?"

"I should have listened to you. I'm sorry."

~~~

Phil parked the car in front of Jamie's garage. Jamie had fallen asleep soon after turning onto the interstate. She began waking up as he parked in her driveway. She looked around wild eyed as if she had woken up in a strange world. "You're home," Phil told her.

Jamie stretched as her awareness returned to her. "Can you come in for a few minutes?" she asked him.

"Sure," he answered. "I can come in for a couple of minutes." He smiled at her in a conscious effort to shed some light into her darkness. She managed a weak smile in return.

Phil exited the car and met her at her door as she opened it. He held out his hand to her. She took it and let him help her out. She pulled the house key out of her front jean pocket as they walked around to the front entrance. She opened the door and began leading Phil in when she stopped so abruptly that Phil bumped into the back of her.

Phil looked over her shoulder into the front living room of the house. Items were scattered across the floor. Picture frames with broken glass, slashed seat cushions with their stuffing pulled out and various knick-knacks were spread out in all directions. Furniture had been turned over and lay at odd angles as if someone had violently thrown them into the room.

Jamie audibly gasped. She turned, bumped hard into Phil and turned back again. She took one step deeper into the living room turned again, ran into Phil's chest again and then slid around him to exit the house.

Phil stepped in. He flicked the light switch on, but no lights came on. He let his eyes adjust to the dim light coming in through the open door and leaking in around the curtains. He looked around. Everything he could see appeared broken, smashed, or ripped open. Fist sized holes had been knocked in walls. He could see the refrigerator, lying face down with its doors spread wide open. Its contents had been strewn around the kitchen and milk had pooled around it. Lying on the back of the refrigerator was Sheba, lifeless, with her neck twisted at an unnatural angle.

He turned around to see Jamie standing several feet away from the house on the sidewalk. She held both her hands to her face, her eyes expressed her horror. Phil hurried quickly back to Jamie. He held his arms out to her. She folded into his arms and began to sob.

"It's OK," he told her. "We'll call the police and they can find out who did this. It's OK."

~~~

They waited outside on the sidewalk as the police checked each room, looking to see if anyone was still in the house. The female police officer signaled them both from the doorway to join her inside. As they entered the male police officer acknowledged them with a nod and returned to making notes in a notepad.

"We don't see any sign of forced entry," the female officer told them. "Do you know of anyone else who has a key?"

"Only my mother," Jamie replied.

"What about your boyfriend?" she asked as she nodded towards Phil.

"No. We're just friends."

"Do you have a spare key hidden somewhere outside?"

"No."

The cop turned her head and looked over the carnage. "It looks like they were either looking for something or this was just malicious destruction. Do you have anything that someone may have been looking for?"

"No," she said. "They killed my cat. Why would someone do that?" She fought to say the words as her throat clenched with emotion.

"I don't know, Ma'am."

Jamie wiped her eyes again with a tissue and tried to regain her composure.

"No cash in the house, drugs or guns?" the cop asked.

"No," Jamie replied. "Oh wait! I have a pistol that I inherited from my grandfather."

"Where do you keep that?"

"In a locked box in my bedroom closet."

"OK," the cop said. "Let's see if we can find it."

They moved into the master bedroom. Jamie looked over the destruction in her bedroom for the first time. Nothing was left untouched or undamaged. She immediately found the wooden box that the pistol had been kept in. It lay open in the middle of the floor. Jamie picked it up and showed the officer. "This is where I kept it."

"What kind of pistol was it?"

"A revolver."

"Do you know the make and model?"

"No. I've only had it a couple of years. I've never shot it."

"Is its registration current locally?"

"Yes."

"OK," the cop responded, as she made a note in her own notebook. "I can find the information by checking the registration."

"No drugs in the house?" The officer repeated the earlier question.

"No."

"Cash?"

"No."

"And just to clarify where you were last night, where were you?"

Jamie gave Phil a worried look. Phil gave her a nod. "I was in Jail," she said quietly as she looked down at the floor.

"Jail?" the cop asked. "Why were you in jail?"

Without looking up she said quietly, "I violated a PPO."

"Who took out the PPO?"

"My half-brother," Jamie told her.

"Would you think your brother would want to do this to you?"

"Half-brother," Jamie corrected. "Maybe."

"Half-brother," the officer said. "Why did he take out a PPO against you?"

"Because we have a disagreement about whether I should be allowed to see my father or not."

"So, you think your half-brother did this because he's mad at you for trying to see your father?"

"I didn't say that, but, yeah," Jamie said. "He's the only person I can think of that would do this."

"OK," the officer said. "What's his name?"

"David St. James," Jamie told her.

The officer began writing the name down in her notebook when she stopped and looked up at Jamie. "That name sounds familiar," she said.

"He's the CEO of Tashe International."

"Hmm," the cop hummed as she looked back down at her notepad. "OK."

The officer finished writing the name in her book. The left side of her face made a quick smirk and then relaxed again. "OK, Ms. Fulton," she said as she slipped the notepad into her right front shirt pocket. "We'll contact Mr. St. James to see if he has anything to say." She waved her arm directing Jamie and Phil out of the bedroom as the two of them exchanged glances.

They stepped into the living room where the male police officer was more closely examining some of the damage. "Will you go through the house one more time with me before you leave?" Jamie asked her.

The officer exchanged a look with her male partner. He gave her a curt nod. "OK," she told Jamie. "The bedroom's clear. Let's start in the basement."

Jamie had not seen the basement yet. The destruction was equal to anything that had been done upstairs. Boxes of stored clothing had been ripped open and their contents were strewn everywhere. Powdered laundry detergent was covering everything. Several items of clothing were ripped or shredded. Anything that had any value at all seemed to be damaged beyond any further use.

The rest of the house was no better but the tension in Jamie eased as the police officer went with her room to room to prove that no one else was still in the house.

The male police officer held out a business card to Jamie. "This is my card. Feel free to call me if you can think of anything." He turned the card over. There was a number written in black ink on the back. "This is the case number. You can pick up a copy of the report at the police department tomorrow. Your insurance will want to see it."

Jamie took the card. "Thank you," she said.

"Do you two live here together?"

"No," she answered, as she shot a quick glance at Phil standing next to her. "We're just friends."

"OK," he said. "I might suggest that you put an alarm system in. Perhaps get a dog." He turned and began to follow his partner out of the house.

"Thank you," Jamie said.

"You're welcome," the male officer said without looking back at her.

Jamie stood in the doorway and watched as the two cops climbed in their car. The female officer sat in the driver's seat. They remained there for several moments.

A sinking sensation in Jamie told her that the cop had not believed her about David St. James being her half-brother. The cop's almost imperceptible smirk gave that away. Nothing more was going to be done by the police. She was certain of that. They took no fingerprints and only a few pictures. Jamie could not help but narrow her eyes in resentment at the two cops parked in her driveway. Her whole life was now in ruins, and her home was destroyed. The two people who were supposed to help her did nothing at all. She wished they would leave, get out of her sight. They were making her angry, just sitting there, doing nothing. She hated them. Get a dog. Get an alarm system. How about get the people that did this to me? How about actually talking to David St. James. How about I get another gun? If whoever did this walked in the door again, I'll put holes in them, half-brother or not.

The police cruiser began pulling out of the driveway. Jamie snapped alert as if waking out of a dark day dream. She shook her head to clear her thoughts.

"Are you OK?" Phil asked her.

"Yeah," she answered. "I'm fine."

She closed the front door behind her, turned and looked over what remained of her once comfortable home. She walked to the refrigerator and looked down at the cat. "They killed Sheba," she said as she gently stroked its fur with the back of her fingers. Tears rolled slowly down her cheeks. "Why would someone kill a cat?"

Phil stood beside her, wrapped an arm around her shoulder and pulled her tightly to himself. "Some people are just evil," he said.

"I have to bury her," she said quietly.

"Do you want to wait until tomorrow?"

"No. I should do it now."

She wrapped the cat in a towel and took her outside. Phil had found a shovel in the garage and dug a small hole in the inside edge of the back of her yard. Jamie gently placed the bundle in the hole and stroked it once with her fingertips. "Good bye, Sheba," she said. "I'll see you on the other side."

She stood and let Phil bury Sheba. She was no longer crying but her face was hollow, her eyes empty. When Phil finished, he wrapped an arm around her shoulders again and squeezed her. She looked up at him. "Thank you," she said.

"You're welcome," he replied. "I am really sorry."

"Me too. I wish I had never heard of the name St. James before."

They walked together into the house. "I don't know where to start," she told Phil.

"It's almost one o'clock," Phil told her. "You haven't had any sleep for at least thirty-some hours. How about we just hold off on doing anything more right now? If you'd like, you can come over to my place so you can get some sleep. You can stay as long as you need to while you get things taken care of here."

Jamie looked up into Phil's face. Everything about him showed his concern for her. She looked around her home again and nodded a weak yes.

~~~

Phil led her into his apartment and into the living room. "Are you hungry?" he asked.

"No, thank you."

"You can have the guest room upstairs if you want to get some sleep. The bed's all made up."

Jamie did not respond. She moved slowly towards the sofa and sat down on one end of it. Her feet were flat on the floor in front of her. She placed her hands palms down in her lap and let her eyes rest on the floor as they began to tear up again.

Phil sat down beside her, placed an arm around her and squeezed her tightly. She rested her head on his shoulder and broke down in sobs. Phil took her hand with his free hand and gave it a gentle squeeze as he held her in a sideways hug.

"Why?" Jamie asked. "Why would someone do this to me?"

"I don't know," Phil replied softly.

"First, I'm arrested and then this."

Phil only squeezed her hand.

They sat together for a few minutes until Jamie had cried herself out. "Would you like something to drink?" he asked again.

"Can I have some water?"

"Sure. I'll be right back."

He returned moments later with a tumbler of cool water. She took several swallows and handed it back to him. He set it on the end table.

"Can I use your shower?" she asked.

"Sure. There's a bathroom upstairs next to the guest room. You can use that one while you're here."

"Thank you," she said. She moved slowly as she tried to stand from the sofa. Phil held out his hand to her and helped her up. She winced as she tried to break through her body's stiffness.

Phil guided her to the guest room and then showed her the bathroom.

"Phil?" she said as she looked up at him. "I don't have any clothes. What I'm wearing has pepper spray in it."

Phil seemed to blush for a moment. "Well," he said uncomfortably. "It seems a bit cliché, but would you want to use one of my dress shirts?" Jamie gave him a weak smile. "Ok, I'll bring you a couple."

Phil waited for her while sitting at the counter in his kitchen. When she reemerged, she stood at the end of the hallway, barefoot, wearing one of his Oxford dress shirts. Her hair was still damp, but it was combed out nicely. She looked at him shyly.

"Feel better?" he asked her.

"Yes," she answered. "Thank you."

"You're welcome. You hungry yet?"

"No, not really."

"OK, let me know when you are, and I'll make you something. Or," he added, "you can just dig into the fridge yourself, if you would like."

"Thank, you," Jamie said as she walked slowly into the living room. She sat down on the sofa with her feet curled up under her. Her skin was pale with deep, dark circles under her eyes. She stared vacantly toward the floor and absent mindedly combed her hair with her fingers.

"Phil?" she said. Phil took two steps toward her from where he stood in the kitchen. She glanced up quickly into his face, then turned her eyes downward again.

"Yeah?" he said.

She made a quick glance at his face again. Without looking up, she asked, "Can you hold me for a little while?"

She looked up to gauge his reaction. He smiled softly and nodded. He sat beside her, sliding in between Jamie and the arm of the sofa, wrapped his arm around her and gave her a gentle squeeze. She rested her head on his shoulder and settled into his embrace. Within seconds, she was asleep.

Ralph Nelson Willett

Chapter 14

"Wow," the alarm system tech said as he looked over the carnage that used to be Jamie's home. "Did they catch who did this?"

"Not yet," she replied. "I don't think the cops are even trying. I'm not that important."

"Well, the new security system will help," he said. "You'll be able to see live video of all the main living spaces and all three external doorways."

"That's good," Jamie said, as she furrowed her eyebrows and nodded.

"Our security center will see what you see, and we can have the cops here before any more damage is done."

"I'm not really worried about the damage, so much," she told him. "What would have happened if I would have been home?"

The tech nodded. "The entire house is alarmed now. You know where all the panic buttons are. We can have someone here in minutes."

Jamie shook her head and looked over the destroyed items scattered around her living room. "Minutes," she repeated. "Maybe I wouldn't have minutes."

The security tech bit the side of his lip and nodded back. "We can take care of you," he promised.

"I hope so," she replied.

He took her around to each entry point in the house and reviewed the alarm panels with her. He walked with her through the house and around the outside, pointing out each security camera. After returning inside, the tech called the security center with his cell, gave them a code and notified them that he was doing a test. While on the call with them, he pressed the panic button. Her cell phone rang almost immediately. "Answer it," he told Jamie. "They'll ask for your code. Be sure to give them the right one."

Jamie answered the call. "This is Falcon Security," the female voice said. "A panic button has been pressed. May I have your code?"

"Day Dreamer," Jamie responded.

"Thank you," the woman said and disconnected the call.

"They won't tell you if you answered correctly or not," the tech said. "If you say the wrong thing, they'll dispatch."

"OK," Jamie said.

Jamie signed the paperwork and watched through the front
window as the security technician backed his van out of the
driveway and drove off. It nearly depleted her savings
account, but it did make her feel better to have a new
security system.

She turned and looked over all the broken things that she
once thought made her house a home. The insurance
adjuster came in the day before and looked over the
damage. He was a stern man in his late fifties whose face
seemed to be frozen in a permanent frown. He asked very
few questions. "How did they get in? Where were you? Is
there someone you suspect that may have done this?" It
was all in the police report and Jamie knew he had already
reviewed it, but she answered his questions. He did not bat
an eye at the fact she had been in jail at the time the break-in
happened. He took what seemed like hundreds of pictures
throughout the house and even on the outside where there
had been no damage. In the end, he declared that her
insurance would cover the entire contents of her house as
well as all the damage to the walls and fixtures, less her
deductible. He felt that there was nothing worth trying to
salvage. He even agreed to pay for the dumpster rental she
would need to dispose of everything. As he left, he told her
he would have a check for her in about five business days.

She noticed the broken frame that held a picture of her and
her grandfather. She stepped over the debris to cross the
room and gently picked it up off the floor. The wooden
frame was split open at one corner and the glass was broken
into long shards. The picture looked like someone had
stabbed it multiple times with a knife.

Anger began to boil again inside her. She pulled out her cell and dialed Curt Linden for the third time that day and for what seemed like the thousandth time since she was arrested four days ago. Again, there was no answer and no voice mail box. She disconnected the call and fought to suppress the urge to throw the phone hard against the wall.

She blamed Curt for getting her arrested. He was the one who had convinced her to violate the restraining order. He had told her to call him if she needed him. He was her first call from the county jail. He did not answer. Now, she was not sure why she wanted to talk to him at all. Did she want to blame him directly, to tell him how much damage he had caused to her life? Or did she just want someone to scream at? Why had she been such a fool to trust anything that man had said? It had already been several days since she swapped out the Coznephidone for aspirin. Wouldn't she have heard something by now if it had worked? It did not matter. She had no intention of seeing Brett St. James again. There was no point. Her father did not want to know her as she grew up. Why bother now? There was nothing that he had that she wanted from him, not his money, not a relationship and not a half-brother.

She clenched her teeth. David St. James was the one that took out the restraining order against her. He was the one who lied to the court saying she threatened her father. He was the one who had called her mother a whore. He was the one who threatened her and her mother. He was responsible for the break in.

A knock came at the front door, shaking her out of her thoughts. Her heart raced as she spun towards the door wild eyed. Every noise in the house now terrified her. She forced herself to take a deep breath, made her way through

172

the debris and peered through the peep hole. She was relieved to see her mother standing outside.

"Hi, Mom," she said as she opened the door to her.

"Hi, Hon," Carol Ann replied, as she gave her a quick hug. Jamie attempted to guide her in, but her mother froze at the door.

"Oh, my gosh!" Carol Ann said. She stood aghast as she looked over all the smashed and broken pieces that once were the things and treasures of her daughter's life. Jamie had told her over the phone what had happened, but the damage was far greater than she ever imagined. "Oh, my gosh," she said again.

Jamie gave her a moment to look over the ruins. "Everything," Jamie said.

"Is there anything left?" Carol Ann asked her daughter.

"They even squeezed the toothpaste onto the floor." Jamie guided her in, closed the door and locked it behind them. "Careful where you walk. There's glass everywhere."

Her mother held her hand to her chest as she looked around. She stepped carefully to the master bedroom door. "You're not staying here at night, are you?" her mother asked.

"No. A friend from work is letting me use a spare room for a while."

"Was anything stolen?"

"As far as I can tell, the only thing missing is Grandpa's old pistol."

Carol Ann walked deeper into the bedroom. Trash crunched under her feet. The mattress had been leaned against the wall. It was sliced open in a large crisscross 'X'.

"You can't stay here," her mother gasped.

"Everything is getting replaced. The alarm system installer just left."

"No. I mean you can't stay here." Carol Ann turned to look at her. "Whoever did this was out to get you. This was personal. They know where you live. I'm afraid for you."

Jamie shook her head and looked down at the floor. "I'm not going to let someone run me out of my home."

"What would have happened if you would have been home? They could have killed you."

"I don't think they would have been able to do this if I had been home."

"That doesn't make sense," her mother said in exasperation. "You were lucky you weren't home. You were lucky you were in jail." She turned her head looking over the damage. "Look, you can stay with me rent free until you can sell this place and get a new one."

"I'm not leaving, Mom. I love this neighborhood. I worked hard to buy this place. I'm not leaving it."

"Then what are you going to do?"

"I'm staying. I'll get everything fixed up and replaced and then move back in."

"But…" her mother began to protest.

"Mom," Jamie interrupted, "you're the one that keeps telling me to trust God. I'm going to trust him to keep me safe."

"Don't lay that on me, Jamie," her mother retorted angrily. "I never told you to not use common sense. You don't know who did this. They could come back or they could be stalking you. You have no idea why they did this. I know I said to trust God, but the Bible also says to be wise. Staying here isn't wise."

Jamie stood quiet for a moment. "I think I do know who did this, or at least who's responsible for it."

Carol Ann cocked her head to one side. "Who?"

"David St. James."

Carol Ann took a deep breath and let it out. "Because he wants you to stay away from Brett?"

"Yeah."

Carol Ann visibly released the tension that had been building in her and spoke more softly. "I knew Brett fairly well at one time. He was a good guy. He wouldn't have ever done anything like this. But I have no idea about David. I haven't seen him since he was maybe six or seven years old. I don't know what he's capable of doing."

"He's not a nice guy," Jamie told her.

"What makes you say that?"

"I had a conversation with him," Jamie answered. "He said some bad things and threatened me. Then he took out that restraining order."

"How did he threaten you?"

"Oh," Jamie looked out of her bedroom window. "He just said that he would make our lives a living hell."

"Ours?"

"You and me."

"Jamie, Hon, you need to stay away from them. We've been just fine without them. I know you wanted to know who your father was, but this isn't worth it."

"I know."

"So, please, move back home and sell this place. Maybe you can find a place closer to me."

Jamie looked at the floor and nodded. "Let me think about it." She looked up and smiled at her mother. "I could get a big dog."

"I'm sorry about Sheba," her mother said sadly.

"Me too," Jamie replied. "The man is just evil."

~~~~~

Five friends, four from work, a neighbor and her mother had volunteered to help her clean out her house so that the contractors could come in and repair the damage. Four men, including Phil, carried the destroyed things out to the two dumpsters parked in Jamie's driveway. Three women assisted Jamie with sorting through the debris looking for anything that was salvageable. The more items that were cleared, the more damage became evident. Even electrical wiring in the basement had been cut. It might have been easier if St. James would have simply burned the house down.

All the large items needed to be dragged to the dumpsters and tossed in. Two large trash cans were used to carry out the smaller debris. They used wide flat tipped shovels to fill them. Very little was salvageable. Some pots and pans from the kitchen were spared along with most of the silverware. Most of the drinking glasses had been broken. Even some of her old college textbooks were ripped apart. Whoever did this, took their time. They were thorough.

Jamie took a drink from a plastic water bottle on the counter. Phil had brought a cooler full of ice and bottles of water with him. She lowered the bottle and wiped the sweat from her forehead with the short sleeve of a new Cleveland Browns T-shirt. Her cell rang. She pulled it from her back pocket and read the caller ID. It was Curt Linden.

She gritted her teeth in a flaring anger. Her world faded away to a single focus as she stared hard at the name on the screen. She had finally given up on calling Linden. She had lost count of how many times she had tried. But now here he was, calling her almost a week after she needed him. She hit the answer button hard and held the phone firmly against her ear. She walked quickly to the kitchen window and faced outward toward the street. Her attention was solidly fixed on Curt Linden.

"What do you want?" she said angrily into the phone.

"Hi, Jamie." Linden's voice was soft and gentle. "I heard what happened. I'm sorry."

"Where were you?" Jamie shouted into the cell. "You said to call you if I was arrested and you'd bail me out. You said I *wouldn't* be arrested!"

"I'm sorry, Jamie," Linden said soothingly. "I was in the ICU. I had a heart attack just after we last spoke. I just came home late yesterday."

Jamie's anger slowly began fading away. She had trusted him. She had counted on him. But things outside of his control had intervened. The tension began to ease.

"Jamie," Linden said. "Are you OK?"

"I was arrested. They pepper sprayed me." Her voice remained loud and angry.

"Pepper sprayed? Why?"

"I don't know. The cop put handcuffs on me and kept yelling for me to stop resisting and then sprayed me right in the eyes. I wasn't resisting."

"I am so sorry, Jamie," Linden said. "There has to be another reason they'd do that."

"They didn't need to do that," Jamie said. "I wasn't resisting. He was just an evil cop."

"So, do you have to go back to court?"

"Yeah, but I don't have a court date yet."

"I'm sure you'll be fine."

Jamie instantly tensed again. "You're sure?" she said, voice rising. "You were sure I wouldn't be arrested. You said they'd just give me a warning. You talked me into going back to check on Brett. You did this to me!"

"Jamie…" Linden began.

Jamie interrupted, "You!" she shouted angrily into her cell. "You did this!"

"I am so sorry," Linden said using his soothing voice. "I wish that hadn't happened."

"You!" she shouted again. "My life is in ruins because of you!"

"Jamie, please. I need to tell you something."

"Good bye, Curt!" Jamie said angrily. "Don't call me again." She began pulling the cell away from her ear.

She nearly missed what Linden said next. "Brett is better!" She froze and held the phone against her ear again. "Jamie," Linden said. "He's asking for you."

Chapter 15

Jamie stood silent. Her mind fought to put the pieces together. Brett was better. Why did that surprise her? That was the entire intent of swapping the Coznephidone with aspirin, but to hear that it worked caught her off guard.

"Jamie?" Linden prompted. "You still there?"

"Yeah," she answered quietly.

"He's asking for you."

"I heard you."

"He wants to see you."

Jamie's eyes darted around the room as thoughts raced through her mind. She caught Phil looking at her, he tilted an ear towards her and furrowed his eyebrows. Locking eyes with him, she calmed herself and took a deep breath. "I still have a restraining order out against me. I can't go see him."

181

"I think that can be fixed," Linden told her. "I'll talk to David, but you need to go see Brett before David does. I don't know what he'll do if he sees Brett is in his right mind. He's the one that put him on the drug in the first place."

"I can't risk going back there, Curt. I've already been arrested once."

"Jamie…"

"When did you talk to him?" Jamie interrupted.

Linden hesitated before answering. "About ten minutes ago. Just before I called you."

"Did you go see him?"

"No. He called me."

"He has a phone?" Jamie asked suspiciously.

"He called me from Ruth Markham's phone."

"Who's that?"

"She's the woman who chased you out of the church. Her and her son. She called me to let me know what was going on and then let me talk to Brett. He wants to see you."

"You said that," Jamie said. "I'm not going anywhere near that church until David takes the restraining order off me. Have David call me."

Linden hesitated again. "Jamie, I can't have David call you. I told you why. If he finds out that Brett is in his right mind, who knows what he'll do."

Jamie's chest tightened. The muscles in her jaw tensed. "What is it that you think I can do, Curt? If I go see him, I'll be arrested again. I'm not going to do that. You'll have to find another way. I'm not doing it."

"Jamie, I'm sorry for what happened. I honestly didn't think you'd be arrested. I was wrong. I'm sorry."

"Yeah, Curt," Jamie said harshly. "Your being wrong got me pepper sprayed and put in jail. And you weren't there to help when you said you would."

"I was in the hospital," Linden protested.

"It doesn't matter," Jamie retorted sharply. "It's because of you I'm in this whole mess. I've been arrested, pepper sprayed for no reason and my home was destroyed. You've already admitted that the whole letter thing was just a ruse. I have less reason to trust you than I do David. At least David is being honest."

"But David…"

"David is going to find out soon enough that Brett is in his right mind," Jamie interrupted. "I'm not your hero. I can't deal with all this."

"Jamie…"

"I was desperate to know who my father was. I'm not now. I've met him. I know who he is. Now, I know that he didn't think it important enough to meet *me* for thirty years. He didn't need me then. I don't need him now. What I need is for you to leave me alone. I'll go see him when David calls me and asks me to."

"OK," Linden said. "I'll talk to David. Let's see if I can talk him into removing the restraining order."

"You do that," Jamie told him. "Until then, don't call me anymore."

She angrily disconnected the call and looked up to see everyone had gathered in front of her. "What's going on?" Phil asked her.

"That was Curt Linden," she told them. "He said my father was better and asking for me. But something doesn't feel right. I can't put my finger on it, but something feels wrong."

~~~~

"I screwed up," Bob Kinross said of his alter ego, Curt Linden, as he hung up the call with Jamie. Kinross paced slowly back and forth behind his Chevy SUV. He kept his hands in his front pockets and his head down, deep in thought. The call did not go as he expected. He blew the trust he had built up with Jamie. Maybe, had he actually bailed her out of jail, he would still be able to control her, but that would have exposed who he really was, Bob Kinross, and not who he pretended to be, Curt Linden.

"Why?" asked the deputy leaning back on the hood of his cruiser with his arms crossed, watching Kinross pace. They had met several times like this, always on slow, back roads. If anyone happened by, they would only see a sheriff's deputy talking to some old man he had pulled over. It would be unlikely that anyone would notice who they were. No one would remember them, no record of a traffic stop, and no way to connect them. "What happened? Is your little ruse falling apart?"

"Maybe I shouldn't have had you arrest her," Kinross said without looking up.

"We had to," the deputy replied. "We needed to establish that she was willing to violate a PPO and was being aggressive and hostile."

"I know, I know," Kinross said with a dismissive wave of his hand.

"But tearing her house up was a mistake for sure. We didn't need to do that."

The deputy grinned. "But it was a lot of fun."

Kinross stopped pacing and stared hard at him. His eyes narrowed, and his jaw clenched. "You didn't need to kill her cat," he shouted at him.

"I said it was a lot of fun," the deputy replied as he shrugged his concern. "So yeah, I did."

Kinross held the stare for a moment, nodded, spit on the ground and continued pacing.

"Besides," the deputy added. "We have her pistol now."

"She doesn't trust me anymore," Kinross said. "I didn't plan for that. I thought she'd accept the explanation that I had a heart attack. I've got to get her back in the church somehow. We're so close. Everything was going exactly as planned but now she doesn't want to see Brett again."

"Why not just drag her there?" The deputy asked.

Kinross froze and looked up at the deputy.

"Just call her up and tell her you'd like to meet her for dinner. Tell her that Brett will be coming with you. Then force her into the car and take her to the church. I can come with you, so we can bring her car to the church."

"I don't think she'll take my calls anymore." Kinross looked down and kicked at a stone in the gravel. "Maybe I can talk David into rescinding the PPO. He's been pretty pliable up to this point. Then he can call her and let her know it's OK to come."

"No," the deputy replied curtly. "She has to be in violation of the PPO again when this all goes down. You spent a lot of time talking David into taking it out in the first place."

"Yeah. I know. I can't have David call her anyhow. I already told her that Brett called me and that he's better. If she asks David about him, he'll ask what she's talking about. It'll be hard to explain why Brett really isn't any better. "

"Then we're back to snatching her."

"Maybe," agreed Kinross. "Let me think about it for a while. I'll let you know."

"OK, Uncle Bob. It's your show. Call me when you're ready."

The deputy walked back to his driver's side door, climbed in and turned off the police lights. He waved his hand at his uncle as he drove off, kicking up a cloud of dust behind him.

Ralph Nelson Willett

Chapter 16

Jamie and Phil sat cross-legged facing each other in the middle of her living room floor. The opened wine bottle stood upright between them as they each nursed the drink from red plastic cups. Their voices echoed through the empty house. What little was salvageable was stacked on the kitchen island.

"You're looking better," Phil told her.

Jamie chuckled. "Better than what?"

"You don't look quite so pale, so defeated, I guess."

"Yeah. Thanks," Jamie replied. "I think I am feeling better. I don't know what I would have done without everyone's help. I really appreciate what you and everyone else has done."

"I'm glad we could help out."

Jamie took a sip of her wine. "It's like starting over," she said.

Phil nodded. "I'm sorry."

"It's not your fault. I just wish I had never heard of Brett St. James. Things would be a lot easier."

"You really think his son did this?"

"I think it was supposed to be a warning. Why else would anyone do this? The only things missing were my grandfather's gun and that carving Brett made. I didn't have any cash in the house. What would be the point of destroying everything?" She waved her arm at the living room wall. "I mean, look at it, why would anyone knock holes in the wall and gouge the floors and counter tops like this? It wasn't a robbery. And why take the carving? He was trying to send me a message. He's the one that needs to be pepper sprayed. I just wish I could prove it."

"Well, at least he left the draperies intact," Phil told her with a grin, trying to keep her mood from falling.

Jamie laughed. "Yeah," she said. "Thank God for small favors." She took another sip of wine, became serious and looked around at the house. "Maybe I *should* move. I don't know. I'm wondering if I'll ever feel safe here again. Even with this fancy alarm system I'll always be wondering if someone is after me."

"Where would you move to?"

"My mom would like me to move back closer to her but that would make it a forty-minute commute to work. I like my ten-minute drive."

"I'd be a little worried that if word got out about what happened here, that your property value would fall. It might even affect the whole neighborhood."

"I know," Jamie said. "I like where I live. I don't want to be chased off. That's another reason I'm so done with this whole St. James thing. I'll take the hint and stay away."

They sat silently sipping their wine for several moments. "What will you do if you find that Brett is actually better?"

"I don't know," she shrugged. "I guess it all depends. Maybe he won't even remember that I was there. And besides, he kept away from me all these years. Why would he suddenly want to have contact with me now?"

She drank the rest of her wine quickly and began to stand. Phil quickly stood and offered his hand to help her up. "Thanks," she said. She leaned backward and stretched her back. "I'm stiff now."

"Yeah, me too," Phil replied as he twisted his shoulders side to side. "You ready to go back to my place?" Jamie had been using his spare room for the last week.

"Yeah," she said. "I need a shower."

The short drive back to Phil's apartment was quiet. As Phil parked the car Jamie said, "I still can't put my finger on what feels so weird about that call from Curt. But something isn't right."

191

"Like what?"

"That's just it. I don't know. It doesn't feel right. If Brett was really OK, why would he call Curt rather than David? That is, unless he knew that David was the one that messed him up in the first place."

"Isn't that what you think?"

"I think so. But it was Curt that sent me that letter and signed it with Brett's name. Why? Why not just call me? He had my number. Then he talked me into going back to the church after the PPO was taken out against me." She shook her head. "I should have known better than that one. I feel so stupid."

"Don't blame yourself for that one. You were talked into it," Phil told her sympathetically.

"But I *knew* better," she insisted. "Even you warned me. But for some reason, I let him talk me into it."

"We've all made mistakes. Don't beat yourself up over it."

"No. I'm not," Jamie said. "But there's something wrong. I just wish I knew what it was."

~~~~

It was a misting rain that lasted far too long, making the entire day feel gloomy. Jamie started the day at her house, meeting with the contractors, and then went into the office.

At lunch time she returned to the house again. The walls were being repaired faster than expected and the electricians had already wrapped up and left before she arrived. She expected almost a week for the drywall work to be completed but now she guessed that they may be finished as early as tomorrow. Perhaps, she could have the painters in a couple of days early. Maybe then she could have her new furniture delivered sooner.

Satisfied with the progress, she returned to her office. She was able to see how things were going at her house by watching her security cameras on her cell phone. That was a convenience she had not thought of when she bought the system; the ability to watch how the contractors were progressing from her office desk.

It was still drizzling when she returned home, and the gloominess of the day seemed to settle in for the long haul. She met briefly with the contractors as they cleaned up for the day. All the walls had been patched and just needed a final sanding. That would be completed in the morning. She thanked them as they left for the day.

She had wandered into the basement to check the electrical work when her cell phone rang. She had expected it to be Phil but flushed with anger when she saw that it was Curt Linden. She angrily silenced the ringer and returned the phone to her back pocket. She was walking up the basement steps when her phone chirped to let her know she had a text message. It was from Linden.

"I'm outside," the text said. "I'm in my car parked in your driveway. I need to talk to you. It's important."

Jamie pulled back the curtains of her front room window and saw Linden waiting for her in an old dark blue car in her driveway. "What does he want?" she asked herself out loud. She did not want to talk to him. He saw her looking at him through the window, smiled at her and beckoned her excitedly with his hand.

She stiffened and gritted her teeth. What was he doing here? She had told him to leave her alone. Angrily, she put her jacket on, pulled the hood over her head, and stepped outside into the misting rain. She approached the car with her arms crossed. Linden rolled the window down and smiled broadly at her. "I've got some good news," he said pleasantly as she approached.

She leaned towards him as she approached the car. "What?" she demanded.

A sharp jab in her left kidney caused her to twist and look over her shoulder. A hand shoved her hard in the middle of her back, pushing her up against the car. "Shut up," a male voice said.

"What's going on?" Jamie asked as the man behind her pulled her cell phone from her back pocket.

"Get in the back seat, Jamie," Kinross, the man Jamie knew as Curt Linden, said sternly. He was no longer smiling. She twisted enough to see that it was a pistol being pushed tightly against her back.

"Curt!" Jamie yelled. "What are you doing?"

The man leaned up and spoke quietly in her ear. "If you shout again, I'll kill you. Do you understand me?" Jamie did not respond. "Do you understand me?" he asked again through gritted teeth. She nodded.

He directed her to the back seat, let her get in, and slid in beside her. "OK," the man said. "Go."

Linden backed the car out of the driveway and began making his way towards the expressway.

"Why are you doing this?" she asked Kinross. He did not respond.

The man grabbed her left wrist roughly and placed a handcuff around it. He reached over her, took her right arm and latched the other cuff to her right wrist. Jamie recognized him. He was the deputy that had arrested, and pepper sprayed her. Now, he was wearing civilian clothes. "Lie down," the man growled as he shoved her onto her side.

"What are you doing?" Jamie asked in a high-pitched voice. "Where are you taking me?"

"Shut up," the deputy said. "Don't make me gag you."

They drove in silence for several moments before Kinross spoke up. "I'm taking you to see Brett," he said.

"Why?" Jamie asked.

"He wants to see you, that's why."

Jamie saw the deputy smirk. She saw him tuck the pistol in his pocket. Her eyes darted around as she looked for an escape. She tried to sit up, but the deputy shoved her down hard again.

"I'm not sure if you St. James kids are just stupid or if I'm just that good."

"Curt, please," Jamie begged.

"I did make a couple of mistakes with you, but it's easily fixed," Linden continued. "Tearing up your house was a mistake. I should have realized that you'd put an alarm system in. That was a mistake on my part. But in the end, it will still be proven that you did it all to yourself."

"You did that to my house?"

"Not me, stupid," he said as he nodded back towards the deputy. "He did."

Jamie looked up at the deputy who smirked back at her.

"Why?" Jamie asked Kinross.

"Why not?" the deputy replied. "I did all that in less than two hours. It was lots of fun. What was most fun…" He leaned toward her. "What I really enjoyed was, ringing your cat's neck." He put one fist on top of the other and twisted them, mimicking the action of breaking her cat's neck.

Jamie was horrified. She swore at him. "Why would you do that? My cat couldn't have hurt you."

The deputy laughed.

Kinross continued. "I'm not sure if the mistake was to tear the place up or not to bail you out. In any case, you were mad at me for all that and I couldn't get you to go back to see Brett."

"Why do I need to see Brett?"

"I told you," Linden said. "He's all better now." He laughed. "Not!" he added with a laugh.

"What?" Jamie asked, her voice pleading.

"You swapped out that drug for aspirin. I swapped it back. He's never going to get better."

"Why?"

"Because you're looking for your inheritance."

"I'm not looking for anything!" Jamie shouted.

"Hey now," Linden said. "There's no need to raise your voice. I can hear you."

"I'm not looking for anything from him," Jamie asserted. "You're the one that made me go see him. You're the one that sent me that letter telling me that I'd learn about my father."

"And you did," he answered. "You met your father."

"Why are you doing this?" she pleaded with him again.

"I've already told you," Linden responded showing his irritation at being asked the same question.

"Please, Curt," she begged. "Just let me go."

"*Please, Curt*," the deputy mocked. He laughed at her.

"You can stop calling me that now," Linden said. "My name is Bob."

They drove in silence for a few minutes before Linden said, "We're getting on the highway in just a second. Cover her. I don't want any truckers looking down and seeing her."

The deputy pulled a blanket out from under the front passenger seat and covered Jamie completely. "Take that blanket off and I'll knock you out. Understand me?" Jamie did not respond. "Understand me?" he shouted at her. The only response was a quiet whimper. "You crying?" he asked mockingly. He laughed again. "Yeah, you understand me, stupid."

The drive seemed much longer than when she drove to the church. Her muscles were starting to cramp as she lay in an awkward position. Her legs ached to be stretched. "Where are you taking me?" Jamie asked.

"I told you," Kinross said. "I'm taking you to see your father at the church."

"What are you going to do with me?"

"Nothing you need to worry about."

"Are you going to hurt me?"

Kinross laughed. "Why would I want to hurt you? Seems to me that you're the one that wants to hurt people."

"I don't want to hurt anyone."

"Sure, you do. You threatened Brett. You threatened David. You threatened me. You're going to threaten deputy Kinross here with your grandfather's gun."

She was silent for a moment. "I haven't threatened anyone," she said in a weak voice.

"Not according to the police. Apparently, you're a psychopath."

"Why are you doing this?" Her voice was subdued and quiet.

"Because I'm sick of working for you St. James people," Kinross said angrily. "I'm sick of building up a business and getting nothing to show for it. I'm sick of Brett and David getting rich off what I've done. I'm going to fix that. I'm making things right."

"What have I got to do with it?"

"You still don't get it," he answered. "You're the one that's going to make it all happen."

"You *are* going to hurt me," Jamie whimpered from under the blanket. Kinross did not respond.

"Shut up," the deputy said calmly.

They rode in silence. A few more minutes passed before Jamie felt the car turn off the pavement. She could hear gravel crunching beneath the tires and the car shook as it passed over small, washboard bumps. They drove for a couple of minutes before the car slowed and turned onto a quiet road. The car bounced as if the road was deeply rutted. They pulled to a stop.

"OK," Kinross said. "Go change. I've got her."

Jamie heard the rear door open. The car rocked as the deputy climbed out and closed the door behind him. She pulled the blanket below her eyes and saw Kinross grinning at her. He had his right arm resting on the center console. His hand was gloved. In it was her grandfather's pistol.

"Are you going to kill me?" she asked him.

"You think too much," he told her.

"Are you?"

"Nah. I'm not going to kill you."

She sat up and let the blanket fall to her lap. Kinross shrugged and allowed it. She looked out the front window and saw an old, faded red barn. The large barn door was slid open to one side. She could see a police cruiser parked inside facing her. The deputy was changing into his uniform in front of it. The surrounding area was overgrown with brush, small trees and tall brown grass. She looked desperately for a house, some place to run for help, but there was nothing but woods in every direction. They were too far off the road for her to see where they came in from.

Kinross was watching his nephew impatiently. He checked his watch, looked back at Jamie and then back at the deputy. Jamie slowly pulled the blanket off her lap and dropped it on the car floor, carefully keeping an eye on Kinross and the deputy who was dressing in the open. Jamie quickly raised her cuffed hands to the door handle, pulled hard and shoved her shoulder into it. The door did not budge. In a fast movement, she attempted to unlock the door. The button was up.

Kinross looked back at her in amusement, as she tried the door handle again. She slid to the other side of the car and tried the opposite door. It did not open either. She screamed in frustration, rolled to her back and kicked at the door with both feet. She grunted loudly with the effort. She kicked at the window with no better result.

She looked angrily at Kinross again. The smirk on his face infuriated her. In a rapid movement, she sat up behind Kinross and reached over his head with both arms and pulled back hard against Kinross's neck with the links of the handcuffs. Kinross gasped in surprise, gagged and fought to put his free hand between the handcuffs and his neck. Jamie leaned back with all her weight and put both knees in his seat back to apply more leverage. Kinross attempted to swing the gun around in her direction but let it fall into the passenger seat to free his hand to push against the crushing pressure Jamie was applying to his neck. Jamie grunted loudly as she poured all her strength into the choke. Kinross turned a crimson red. She could feel him weakening.

The door suddenly opened, and the deputy put a pistol against her temple. "I'll kill you here and now," he told her in a calm voice. Jamie slowly loosened her grip. Kinross angrily pushed her arms off his neck and over his head. He coughed several times as he opened his door and nearly fell to his knees climbing out. He paced rapidly back and forth in front of the car as he rubbed his neck, swearing loudly. He stopped pacing, put both hands on the car hood and leaned in towards her. He screamed a stream of profanities at her as he hammered both fists down hard on the car hood multiple times.

Jamie looked back and forth between Kinross and the gun pointed at her head. She was panting angrily, glaring at the deputy. "Get out of the car," he told her. Jamie began moving slowly, her vision fixated on the deputy's gun. He gripped her by the shoulder of her jacket with his free hand and pulled her out roughly. She stumbled forward a few paces but remained standing. Turning, she saw the deputy scowling, arm stretched out, pointing the gun directly at her head. She winced and closed her eyes against the expected gun shot. It did not come. As she opened her eyes again, she saw Kinross charging at her. He grabbed her by the throat with his left hand and cocked his right fist, preparing to hit her.

"Stop!" the deputy ordered loudly. Kinross froze in place with his fist pulled back to strike. His face was contorted with anger, the muscles in his neck and face were taut to the point that his head shook. "There can't be any marks on her," the deputy said loudly. It was a moment before Kinross released his grip on her. He snapped away as he turned his back towards her and took a few steps. Jamie breathed in gasps. Kinross walked away angrily, swearing loudly.

"Get the gun," the deputy ordered Kinross. Kinross stopped and glared hard at Jamie for a moment as he fought to regain his composure. He leaned in through the driver's side door and retrieved her grandfather's pistol from the passenger seat. He stood up outside of the car, the pistol hanging down at his side. He looked calmly at Jamie for a moment, then raised the pistol, pointing it at her head. He cocked the hammer.

Jamie flinched with a terrified squeal, hunched her shoulders as she ducked her head and turned her back to him. Again, the expected shot did not come. She slowly turned her head and looked around her shoulder at him. The barrel of the gun gaped at her. Kinross's eyes flared. His face was steeled and determined.

"Let it go," the deputy said calmly to him. Kinross took a step closer toward Jamie and stiffened his arm holding the pistol. Jamie closed her eyes and looked away. "Stop!" the deputy yelled. Kinross froze. "We need her," the deputy told him.

Kinross was breathing hard through flaring nostrils. The fire in his eyes declared his willingness to kill her. He held his pose, as he mentally forced himself back from pulling the trigger. It took a moment before he began pulling back from the brink of ending her life. His shoulder dropped first. He slowly lowered the pistol toward the ground and uncocked the hammer. "We need her," the deputy told him again more calmly.

Kinross swore at her, tucked the pistol in his belt behind his back, turned and walked angrily to the front of the car. He leaned against the car hood, crossed his arms and stared down at the ground with furrowed eyebrows. His chest rose and fell with each angry breath.

The deputy returned his weapon to its holster on his side and finished dressing by tucking his shirt into his pants. "Stupid," he said calmly.

Jamie faced him. "If you're going to kill me, then just do it," she demanded.

"Don't be in such a hurry," he replied. "You've got lots of time." He grabbed her by the shoulder of her jacket again and forced her around to the passenger side of the car. He opened it wide and dragged her closer to it. He took her by her wrist, produced a key and unlocked the cuff. Pushing the open cuff through the door pull, he locked her wrist in it again. He forced her back into the car seat.

She sat twisted awkwardly towards the door and watched as the deputy walked around the front of the car to face Kinross. She could see the deputy calmly talking to him but could not hear the words. His eyes darted toward Jamie every few seconds, ensuring that she remained in place. Kinross was nodding in agreement. They both turned to face her. Kinross's lips rose in a sneer that morphed into a contemptuous smirk.

The deputy checked his watch, said something to Kinross, walked to the barn and climbed into the parked cruiser. She looked at Kinross who was staring at her with wild, hate filled eyes. He mouthed an obscenity at her, walked to the driver's side door and climbed in behind the wheel. He started the car, placed both hands on the wheel and sat motionless for several seconds, staring forward.

"What are you going to do?" Jamie asked. There was no acknowledgement that he had heard her. Jamie asked again. "What are you going to do?" she asked again.

"Shut up," he replied calmly.

Jamie yanked hard on the handcuffs and screamed at him, "What are you going to do?"

Kinross flinched. He hesitated a moment and then hammered both fists down on top of the steering wheel. "I'm going to own Tashe International!" he shouted. "I built that company to what it is today! Now, I'm going to own it!"

"What!?" Jamie shouted. "What have I got to do with Tashe?"

He took a moment to calm himself. "Nothing," he replied. "You're just a means to an end."

"What is that supposed to mean?"

Kinross swore and turned to look at her. He was smirking. "You St. James kids are so stupid, so easily manipulated." He swore again. "This has been a fun game. It's almost over now. It's almost over." He turned away and adjusted his windshield rearview mirror to see her.

"What have I got to do with Tashe?" she asked again.

"You're the key, babe. You're the key."

He put the car in drive and began inching forward. He maneuvered the car around until he faced away from the barn. A two-track dirt drive curved to the right through the trees. Jamie turned to see that the police cruiser was beginning to follow them. They drove slowly, bouncing over deep ruts, until they reached the gravel road, turned left and headed… "Where?" Jamie wondered.

"Where are we going?" she asked.

"To church."

"In Amison?"

"Yep."

"Why?"

"Shut up."

"Why?" she screamed at him.

Kinross flinched. "Shut up!" he shouted back.

Jamie was silent for a moment. The car turned onto a two-lane paved road. In a calm voice she said, "If you don't tell me what's going on, you'll have to kill me now." Kinross did not respond. "I'm not playing," she added. "You're going to kill me anyhow." She watched until she saw the speedometer reach sixty, then leaned against the car door and stretched herself out along the length of the rear seat. She kicked his headrest hard. It slammed against the back of his head. He swore at her, reached between the two front seats and tried to swat her. The car swerved. She kicked it hard again. He swore at her again.

"Stop it!" he yelled.

"Not until you tell me what's going on!" She kicked it again. "The next one will be against your head!"

Kinross hit the brakes and began to slow down. "I'm going to kill you right now!" he said angrily.

"Do it!" She screamed back. She kicked hard at his head. Kinross leaned away from the kick. She missed. She pulled her leg back and kicked hard again and again, narrowly missing his head each time. "Do it! Do it! Do it!" she screamed as she began kicking the headrest again multiple times. "You're going to kill me anyhow!"

"Alright! Alright!" Kinross shouted back. Jamie stopped kicking. As soon as it appeared that Jamie relaxed he let off the brakes and began speeding up again. "Alright!" he said loudly. He swore at her. "Alright."

He cleared his throat. "I knew I should have put you in the trunk," Kinross said. Jamie cocked her foot to strike again. Kinross saw the movement in his mirror. "I built this company," he began. "It was me that held Brett St. James by the hand and walked him through building it up into the company it is. It was me! Without me, he couldn't have done squat. When he took off to care for his wife, it was me that ran the company. David had no clue. I told him what to do, what to say and what to think. It was me! It was my company, and it was Brett that was getting rich off me."

"What does that have to do with me?" she asked angrily.

"When Rene died, Brett planned on coming back to work. The company was running just fine. All that money that he floated to you and your stupid mother, I skimmed quite a bit of that." He laughed. "You have no idea."

"So, you stole from Brett," Jamie said. "You still haven't told me what that's got to do with me."

Kinross did not respond. Jamie cocked her foot back again preparing to strike. "Alright!" he shouted. "Brett was going to come back to the company but when I talked to him, all he could do was mope around. He hung out at that stupid church all the time. That's when I got the idea. I met Doc at the party Brett threw at the church for Rene. I knew it would take some time, but I'd retire a very rich man when it's all done.

"I had heard about the side effects of Coznephidone. Through some connections I was able to get quite a bit of it, a lot of it. I convinced David that his father needed to be put on some anti-depressants and since he was hanging out at the church and Doc was local, Doc could be sure he was taken care of. So, I floated Doc some cash. David never figured out that he wasn't a real doctor." Kinross swore. "He was a medic in the military. Doc was his nickname. I kept a few people lubed with cash and nobody asked any questions." He laughed. "You St. James kids are just plain stupid. All of you are. David convinced Brett to take the meds and I supplied them through Doc. Just a little at first and then more. Doc later told David that Brett wasn't taking the drug anymore. Doc diagnosed him with the onset of Alzheimer's and David never questioned it. We just increased the dosage. The problem was he couldn't remember when to take it, so I created a short little limerick for him. You know, that 'pray, pray twice a day' thing, and taught him to take the drug when he prayed.

Kinross laughed. "Brett was such a religious freak." he added. "He had to pray because he felt so guilty over Rene dying. He actually thought God was punishing him."

"I still don't see what that's got to do with me," Jamie told him angrily.

"I knew Brett never met you in person. Before Rene got sick, he tried to sneak into places you might be, just so he could see you, watch you, that type of thing. When I decided it was time to take the company public, I needed to be sure that everyone was out of the picture, including you."

"I wasn't in the picture until you brought me in," Jamie told him.

"You're in his will, stupid," he said.

In the mirror, Kinross saw Jamie's jaw drop. "I know," he said. "I don't see why either. You didn't know. But that doesn't change it. You got a quarter of the company and David got the other three quarters. David never saw that version of the will. He thinks he's the only one getting anything. I helped craft the will, so I at least convinced Brett that if something happened to the both of you, we'd still need a succession plan for the company or all those people would lose their jobs and their families would starve and all that nonsense. So, I'm in the will. If anything ever happens to you and David, I'd get whatever share of the company that either of you left. I set it up so if you both died, I'd get the entire thing. See what I mean? Stupid."

"So, you're going to kill all three of us?"

"Nope," he said as he grinned in the mirror at her. "You are. Or at least Brett and David. Then the police will have to kill you."

"You said you weren't going to kill me."

"I'm not," he said. "See? Stupid."

"I'm not going to shoot anybody," she said flatly. "Even if you kill me."

"Yes," he said. "You will. Here we've got a crazy woman that David St. James needs to take a PPO out on to protect his father, a woman who trashed her own home in a fit of rage when she found out about it. The same woman that violated the PPO and who violently resisted arrest. You may not pull the trigger, but you will kill them."

Jamie was silent. She could see Kinross watching her in the mirror. It was a few moments before she spoke again. "I knew something was wrong with that phone call. When I told you that my house was destroyed you never even questioned it."

"You didn't happen to tell the cops that it was David St. James that did it, did you? You know, the David St. James that runs Tashe International. You do know how crazy that would sound, right? That would be funny." He looked at her in the mirror and grinned. "But I must say, my nephew said he had a great time. I wish I could have been there. I almost feel sorry for your cat though. I like cats."

"Why did you show up in a wheelchair? What was the point?"

"Because you're stupid. I correctly guessed that you'd let your sympathies override your judgement. You'd trust anything I told you. All because I was in a wheelchair."

"That's stupid!" Jamie said.

"I know," he replied. "But you did exactly what I thought you would. I could have talked you into anything and pretty much did."

"Until yesterday when I told you I wasn't talking with you anymore," she said harshly.

"And so here we are," he said in a mocking tone. "Maybe I did make a mistake. I needed to get you to the church. I wanted you to drive there on your own but I'm OK with picking you up if I have to."

"No one is going to believe I shot anyone," Jamie said.

"Again," Kinross replied, "crazy woman. Everybody dies from your gun." He paused and laughed. "Crazy woman!"

"How you going to explain how I got there? I didn't drive there in my car."

"Not a problem. You stole this car trying to cover your tracks."

"You're evil," Jamie sneered.

Kinross laughed. "And we're here," he said as he stopped the car and put it in park.

Jamie sat up and looked out the window. It had gotten dark outside. Kinross parked in front of the church behind David's white Cadillac SUV. She kicked again at his head. He dodged it, put the car in park, opened the door and rolled out while dodging her violent kicks.

The police cruiser pulled in behind them. The deputy opened her door. Jamie put all her strength into holding the door closed while at the same time screaming for help. The deputy was not able to apply enough leverage on the door to open it. "Roll down her window," he told Kinross.

Kinross leaned in, put the key in the ignition and rolled her window down from the driver's side door. The deputy reached in, took Jamie by the hair and tilted her head back as far as it would go. With his other hand he held his pistol against her nostrils. Jamie's eyes crossed as she looked down at the weapon. "You scream, you run or just plain piss me off, I'll kill you. Got it?" Jamie did not answer. "Got it?" he asked again louder.

"OK," Jamie replied.

He released her hair, retrieved a cuff key and removed the cuffs while holding the pistol pointed at her face a mere inch away from her forehead. He opened the door and pulled her out roughly by her wrist. He stood her in front of him, lowered the gun beside his leg to hide it from view, and held her by her jeans waist band in the small of her back. "Let's go," he said, as he drove his knuckles into her back.

Jamie stepped forward, trying to keep her pace slow. The deputy forced her forward. Kinross moved quickly to get ahead of them to open the heavy church doors. He held the door open as the deputy shoved Jamie inside. She glared at Kinross as she was pushed by him.

Chapter 17

The door made a heavy thud and a metallic click as Kinross let it close behind him. Kinross nodded toward the front of the church to direct his nephew ahead. The deputy holstered his weapon but maintained his grip on Jamie's jeans. They stepped into the sanctuary and began walking forward. Three large candles on the altar provided the only light.

"David?" Kinross called out. Hearing no response, he called out a second time. "David?"

The side door at the back of the stage opened and David appeared followed by Doc. Jamie pulled forward hard against the deputy's grip. He held her only a moment and then released her.

She ran up to meet David on the stage. "David, they're going to kill you."

"What are you doing here?" David demanded of Jamie. "You're not supposed to be here."

She turned and stood shoulder to shoulder with David and faced Kinross and his nephew. "They're going to kill you!"

"What are you talking about?"

"They're planning on killing us and Brett, so they can take over your company!" she shouted excitedly as she pointed at Kinross.

David cocked his head at her and narrowed his eyes. He swore at her. "That's Bob Kinross. He works for me."

"I know, I know," she said rapidly. "But he told me his name was Curt Linden. He told me he's retired, and he's a friend of Brett's. He's the one that sent me the letter telling me to come see Brett. He was in a wheelchair when I met him!"

Kinross stepped closer to the stage. The deputy slid between the second and third pews and moved to the outside aisle. He positioned himself between them and the side door. He rested one hand on his holstered pistol, his left hand behind his back and narrowed his eyes at them.

"He's been giving Brett a bad drug that made him like he is," Jamie continued. "It's a drug called Coznephidone. It's been off the market for over five years because it makes people crazy."

He tilted his head up and looked down his nose at her with a sneer.

"Look, I'll show you," Jamie insisted as she rushed to the front of the altar, knelt and pressed the heads of the cherubs.

There was a snap as the hidden drawer popped out. She looked in and saw that it was empty. She put her hand in and brushed it around, trying to prove her eyes wrong. She stopped and looked up at David who moved in for a closer look.

"What's this?" he asked as he squatted down and examined the drawer. He pushed it in an inch, the tension on the spring resisted lightly until the drawer clicked into place. He looked at Jamie as he mentally tried to grasp what was going on.

"There was a drug bottle in here," she told him in quiet desperation. "Coznephidone. It was originally for depression. But it's a bad drug. I swapped it out for aspirin because Curt, I mean *he* told me to." She pointed at Kinross. "I came back to see if he was better but that deputy," she pointed at Kinross's nephew, "arrested me and pepper sprayed me."

David looked past Jamie and stiffened as he took a quick breath in. His eyes widened. Jamie turned to see Kinross holding her grandfather's gun on them. "He told me he's going to kill you," Jamie said quietly to him as they both stood to face the gun being pointed at them.

"What is this, Bob?" David asked him. They turned to see the deputy glaring at them, still standing in place, one hand on his weapon and one hand behind his back.

"You're looking for this, I assume," Kinross said as he held up a medicine bottle. "Oh, don't worry. He hasn't been missing his meds."

"Where's my father?" David asked him as his voice became steeled.

"You worry too much. We'll find him."

Doc stepped off the stage towards Kinross. "You didn't say anything about guns," Doc said.

Kinross turned the pistol towards Doc's chest and fired once. Jamie screamed. David positioned himself between Kinross and Jamie. He held his arm back, attempting to ensure that Jamie stayed behind him. Doc stumbled forward a step and fell to his knees. The surprised look on his face blanked as he fell forward on the floor. "Shut up, Doc," Kinross said coldly.

Kinross moved a step closer to Dave and Jamie. The pistol now centered on David's chest. David held his eyes on the gun and moved backwards as he directed Jamie toward the church side door.

"You St. James's are so easily manipulated," Kinross said.

"Bob!" David shouted as he took two more steps toward the deputy and the side door. "What are you doing?" He glanced over his shoulder to see the deputy now holding his weapon on them. He tried to maneuver himself in front of Jamie to try to block both shooters.

"Recognize this gun, Jamie?" Kinross asked. "You wouldn't believe how fortuitous it was to find that you had a gun," Kinross said. "It's the same gun that you used to kill Doc, David and Brett. Such a shame."

"I haven't killed anyone," Jamie shouted through her panic.

"Not yet. But you will." He stopped his forward movement. Jamie looked at the cop with pleading eyes. "Have you met my nephew yet?" Kinross asked as he did a quick tilt of his head towards the deputy. "Imagine that. He responds to a PPO violation and finds that you killed everyone. Shame, really."

"Why?" David asked.

"Because, idiot," Kinross sneered. "I built Tashe! There wouldn't be a company if it wasn't for me."

"You won't be able to take over the company," David said in disbelief.

"I'm in the will, stupid!" Kinross shouted back. "Haven't you read the new one? If Brett dies and you and Jamie both die, then I get the whole thing." He swore. "Oh, that's right," he said mockingly, "you didn't know about Jamie. Daddy wanted you to think he was such a good Christian father and would never cheat on your mama with some whore who worked for him." He laughed. "You think I'm going to let some fool like you run the place? Not when it was so easy to set all this up. Doc was the only one besides me who knew about the drug. I got whole cases of that crap when it went into recall. Worked perfectly." He laughed. "Ha! Did you know that he's not even a real doctor? He was a Navy Corpsman. People just called him Doc."

"But you're the one who talked me into doing the IPO," David said. "Why? Why would you want me to take the company public if you were going to do this?"

217

"There's so much money flowing through this company," Kinross said. "You never had a clue. I figured out how to skim money off years ago when Brett did it to pay for his little dalliance in Vegas. I just never closed the spigot. Not a single audit even came close. I'll stop the IPO and re-issue in four or five years. Then I can retire a very wealthy man. Very wealthy."

"I paid you very well," David insisted, "way above market."

"I built this company, you moron! Me!" he shouted, as he took a single step forward. "It was me who held your hand through all this. I walked you through everything. You didn't have a clue to what you were doing! I built this company!"

Kinross's aggressive anger caused David to lower his stance and stretch his arms out trying to shelter Jamie. Jamie put her hand on David's shoulder and moved in closer to him. Kinross held the gun out towards David's chest.

"Now, look what we've got," Kinross said. "A woman who has a Personal Protection Order out against her, returns to shoot the man she was supposed to stay away from."

"You told me to take out that order!" David shouted.

Kinross ignored him. "She shows up, kills the father she never knew, but was obsessed over, a man with Alzheimer's. Then she shoots Doc and her big brother. This was just too easy to set up."

The deputy moved closer.

"You don't have to do this, Bob!" David said.

Kinross raised the pistol another inch and pointed it at David's chest again. "Yes, I do," he said. The gun discharged, striking David in the chest. David bent backwards with the shot and would have fallen to the floor had he not fallen into Jamie. He looked up, twisted toward the deputy and with every ounce of his dying energy launched himself at him. The surprised deputy was knocked backwards to the floor as David tackled him.

Jamie screamed as she ducked down and ran toward the door leading to the basement. The deputy pushed David's body off him, sat up, raised his arm towards his fleeing target and fired. The bullet struck the back of Jamie's arm as she opened the door and ran through it. She fell forward, sliding down the stairs on her chest to the landing. She was dazed, stunned, and in excruciating pain. She attempted to push herself up off the landing, but her left arm refused to move. She curled into a ball, rolled into a sitting position and then pushed off with her good arm. The burning pain in her arm screamed at her. She reached around with her right arm and pulled her useless arm tight to her stomach. She ran towards the workshop and was only steps away from the door when another shot rang out. The shockwave of the bullet brushed her hair forward as it missed her left ear by a fraction of an inch. The bullet hit the back wall of the workshop. She ran through the doorway and slammed the door behind her and rammed it closed with her shoulder. She locked the door handle and stood back and to the side of it, staring at it in terror.

A heavy pounding rattled the thin door. "Jamie," came the teasing voice of the deputy. He called her name in a singsong voice. "Jamie," he sang again. "Can you come out and play?"

Three shots rang out and three holes appeared in the door. "Jamie," he sang. "Are you OK? I hope I didn't hurt you."

Jamie spotted a wooden carving of two dolphins splashing out of the water, picked it up, meaning to use it as a club but discarded it as too light to be of any use. Desperately looking to find anything she could use as a weapon, she saw the round wooden mallet that Brett used for his wood carving and picked it up. She held it above her shoulder, ready to strike.

"I'm coming in now," the deputy sang. The door crashed inward with a heavy boot to the door handle. He walked in almost casually and looked at Jamie just as she swung the hammer at him. He blocked the blow by grabbing her wrist with his left hand and twisting it until she was forced to drop the hammer. He applied pressure to her wrist to bend her over in front of him. He shoved her backward onto the floor and raised his pistol to her chest. "It's been fun, Jamie," he said. "Too bad we don't have time to play some more."

Jamie closed her eyes tightly. A whimper escaped her lips as she waited for the fatal shot. A shot rang out. She flinched hard. A second shot. She heard the bullet hit above her head. Her mind did rapid mental checks to locate where the bullet struck her. She opened her eyes and looked up. The deputy was turning slowly to face back through the open door. His gun was pointed towards the ceiling. His face showed complete surprise. He began to lower his gun to point through the door when another shot rang out. The back of the deputy's head splattered outward. He collapsed limply to the floor.

Jamie was stunned. Her mind raced as she tried to comprehend what had happened. The pain in her arm raged at her, demanding all her attention as she held it tightly against herself.

Brett leaned his head through the open door. He did a quick visual check of the workshop, his gun at the ready. Seeing only Jamie, he kicked the gun out of the deputy's hand.

"Are you OK?" Brett asked Jamie quickly as he took three steps towards her. His eyes were narrow, and completely focused on his task.

Jamie could only nod. Brett nodded in return, turned and ran out of the workshop, leaving Jamie alone with the dead man. His blood pooled beneath his head. It became eerily quiet.

A minute seemed like a lifetime as she waited, not knowing what to do. She removed her jacket and rolled up the left sleeve of her shirt until she could hold it as a compress over her wound. The bullet had passed through the arm, perhaps through the bone. She squeezed the rolled-up band of her shirt sleeve, turning it into a makeshift tourniquet.

She forced herself to stand despite the pain and looked at the slowly spreading pool of the deputy's blood stretching toward her. She put her back against the wall and inched her way toward the door, terrified that the dead man would suddenly jump up and attack her again. Once she reached the door, she ran out as quickly as the throbbing pain would allow.

She slowly climbed the stairs until she reached the door. The lights of the sanctuary had been turned on and the light leaked around and under the edges of the door. Jamie tried to peer under the door from three steps down but could not see anything. She stood on the landing, opened the door slowly and peeked through with one eye. She saw Brett kneeling over David with his back towards her.

She approached Brett slowly. Coming near him, she could see that midway down the center aisle was Kinross, lying in a pool of his own blood. He lay face down with a carving chisel sticking out of his neck.

Tears streamed down Brett's face, as he tenderly stroked David's face with his fingers. Her grandfather's gun lay on the floor beside him. Jamie knelt beside Brett and gently rubbed her hand across his back. They knelt in silence.

Tears began to trickle down Jamie's face as well. A long minute passed before Brett spoke. "This is my son," he said in a choked whisper.

"I know," Jamie replied softly. "He's my brother."

Brett looked at her through tear-soaked eyes. "Yes," he said as he lowered his head and wept.

Chapter 18

Jamie parked her Toyota behind David's Escalade off the edge of the street in front of the church. The presence of the Escalade signaled that Brett was here. She saw Brett sitting on the bench facing Rene's headstone. He was leaning forward with his elbows on his knees, his hands clasped, and his head bowed. Jamie and her mother exchanged glances.

"That's him," Jamie told her.

Carol Ann nodded. It had been Jamie's idea for her mother to come along with her to meet Brett at the church. Carol Ann had reluctantly agreed to go. She had no contact with Brett St. James since she left his company nearly thirty-one years before. She did not know what they would have to say to one another now. Too many years had passed.

"Let's go," Jamie said.

They exited the car and Carol Ann stood momentarily on the grass looking at Brett. The man she once looked up to and so greatly admired now looked sadly diminished. There was no indication that he was aware of their presence. Jamie tugged at her mother's arm and they began walking slowly across the lawn toward the cemetery. They were only a few yards away when Carol Ann stopped them. Carol Ann looked at Jamie sadly. "I'd like to meet with him alone for a little bit if that's OK," she told Jamie.

"Are you sure?"

"Yes," she said as she turned toward where Brett was sitting.

Brett's back was to her. Bright flowers had been laid against the headstone and another bouquet had been laid on the fresh grave next to it. Carol Ann walked through the opening in the low fence, hesitated and then took the few remaining steps until she stood close to the bench where Brett was sitting. "Hi, Brett," she said.

Brett did not turn to look at her. He lifted his head and faced Rene's headstone. "Hi, Carol," he replied. "I thought you might come."

"How are you?" Carol Ann asked.

Brett did not respond. A moment passed. Carol Ann thought he was not going to answer her. "I kept my promise," he said softly.

Carol Ann sat beside him on the bench. She reached her arm around his shoulder and gave him a squeeze. "You did," she said. "Everything you said you were going to do, you did."

Brett dropped his head again. "David's stone isn't ready yet. Another two weeks, I guess," he said.

"Brett, I'm so sorry for what happened," Carol Ann told him. "David was a hero. He saved Jamie's life."

Brett nodded. A moment later he quietly spoke again. Carol Ann quickly realized he was talking about Jamie. "I can't tell you how many times I wanted to tell her who I am. There were so many times I just wanted to wrap my arms around her and tell her I loved her. There were so many times I sat in the back at her school concerts, and at your church. I was so happy to see her, but I always felt like crying afterward. When I saw her graduate from State I was so proud of her." He paused. "But I cried for nearly two days. I so badly wanted to see her. I just wanted to know her. I tried to tell myself I was doing the right thing." He turned and lifted his head towards Carol Ann. "We did do the right thing, didn't we?"

"Brett," Carol Ann said. "I don't know. I honestly don't know. I kept my promise, too. I wanted to tell her who her father was so many times. She would ask and get angry with me because I wouldn't tell her. I wanted to cry then, too. I might have told her if I had known that Rene had passed."

Brett sat up on the bench and looked at the headstone. There was a moment of silence as he and Carol Ann gazed at the pink granite stone with the name Rene St. James carved into it. "Did you ever wonder if God was punishing you for your sins?" he asked. "I do."

"Why would God want to punish you?" she asked.

"Because of what I did to you," he said sadly.

"Oh, Brett," she replied. "No…"

"He took Rene. Now he took my son."

"Brett," she said sympathetically. "I was the one who kissed you. Remember? God isn't punishing you. These are just the hard things in life."

Silence passed between them again as they sat thoughtfully. He nodded towards the stone. "I loved her," he said.

"I know."

"I think she knew about us. I'm pretty sure she knew."

"She loved you."

"Yes," he said. "I never understood why."

"Because she did. You were her husband. You loved her and I'm sure she knew that."

"I just felt so guilty, so conflicted. I wanted to tell her that I had a daughter that I wanted to know, but I couldn't. I just couldn't. I couldn't bear the pain I would see in her eyes." There was a pause before Brett added, "Then she got sick."

Carol Ann watched him as he gathered his thoughts. "I bought this church for her, you know. I wanted her to be happy. She grew up in this church. I was so afraid she was going to die before she got to see it finished but it never occurred to me that I would bury her here." He paused a moment. "I prayed for forgiveness every day. I prayed that

God would spare her. I prayed that God would take me and let her live." He turned to look over his shoulder at the church. "I prayed in that church."

"I hear it's beautiful inside," Carol Ann told him.

He looked back at the headstone. "It wasn't always this beautiful. I made most of those carvings after she died. I don't know how I did all that."

"Do you remember what happened?" she asked him.

"Some," he said. "Most of the time I was in a fog. It feels like I just woke up from a long dream. I'm still having a hard time believing what happened, how many years I lost."

"Do you mind if I ask what happened?"

Brett cleared his throat. He sat quietly for a moment and cleared his throat again. "When Rene got breast cancer, we did all we could. We went to the best doctors and specialist. She had surgeries and chemo, but there came a time when she said she was done. She didn't want to do it anymore. She said it was her time to go, that it was OK. All I could do then was watch her fade away day by day.

"She wanted to come back and see the town she grew up in. She went to church here. When she saw that the church was empty she cried. I bought it for her that next week. I had a crew come in and fix it up for her. It was pretty nice. I think it looked more like it did when she was a kid than it does today. When I gave it to her I had the whole town come in for a potluck. I think that was the happiest I had seen her in a very long time. I can remember looking over at her. She was sitting in a lawn chair just watching everyone have a good time. She looked so frail, but she had such a look of peace on her face. I'll always remember her that way, looking so peaceful. She was beautiful. That's the way I'll always remember her."

Tears began to stream down Brett's face. "I'll always remember that look." He wiped his eyes and continued. "She died two weeks later. I had her buried here, by her church." He pointed briefly to her headstone.

He was quiet again as he gathered his thoughts. "I kept coming back here every day," he said. "I just loved her so much that I needed to be by her. I ended up staying here. I slept on the pews at night and then I'd sit out here on this bench during the day. I remembered it snowed, but I still came out here to sit with Rene. I don't remember when David had the apartment built. I don't remember when I started making the carvings. There is so much that I can't remember. I can remember David showing up with Doc and Bob Kinross."

Brett stopped to look at Carol Ann. "Bob was my CFO, chief financial officer. He worked for my grandfather a couple of years before I inherited the company. He worked for me for several years. He was a liar and manipulative. And he was proud of it. I was growing tired of his games and was about to fire him when Rene got sick. I started turning things over to David, so I could spend more time with his mother. She needed so much help. There were so many hospital visits and tests and treatments. I couldn't fire Bob then because David needed help running the company. I should have known that David wasn't strong enough to control Bob. I think Bob really did a number on him.

"I can remember Doc telling me that I was suffering from depression and he was going to prescribe something to help me. I don't know... I'm pretty sure I *was* depressed. How could I not be? That's when things start getting really foggy. I can just remember that I had to pray twice a day. Then I was supposed to pray three times every Sunday. I don't know how I knew what day Sunday was."

Carol Ann listened as Brett continued. "Doc wasn't even a real doctor. I just found that out the other day. The people just called him doc because that's what they called him in the Navy. The stuff they gave me was bad."

"I heard," Carol Ann said.

"I can remember the day Jamie showed up in the church. I know I had a hard time telling what was real and what was just in my head. I can remember touching her and being surprised that she was real. I was mad because I thought I broke my promise to you."

"Was that when the townspeople threw her out?"

"Yeah, I think so," Brett said. "I can't fault the people here. They were trying to protect me. Bob had them all under his thumb. Who knows what all he told them. He and David were paying several of them a lot of money to clean the church and be sure I was taken care of, so I'm sure money had something to do with it all.

"Then I remember the second time Jamie came. She came with David. I remember that I was carving when she came. I gave her a carving."

"You gave her two carvings," Carol Ann told him. "One was an angel in a graduation gown, it was Jamie. The other was Jamie singing when she was a little girl. Jamie said you made a lot of carvings with her face on them."

"They're all gone," Brett said. "I remember making carvings of Jamie, but they're all gone."

"I heard," Carol Ann said. "She still has one. It's the one of her singing. It was in her office when Kinross destroyed her house."

Brett smiled weakly. "That's good. I'm glad." He paused to gather his thoughts. "The last time Jamie came," he said, "I can remember her telling me not to take the drug. I remember her telling me it was making me sick. I stopped taking it. Bob put them back. I can remember him kneeling in front of the altar. I was still pretty foggy, but I was aware enough to know not to take the drug. I stopped praying then."

"Brett," Carol Ann prompted, "do you know why they did all this?"

"Because Bob thought he could take over the company. Before Rene got sick, I tried to set up a logical line of succession so if anything happened to me the people working for me would still have jobs. At the time I set it up, it made sense to have David take over ownership of the company. Bob talked me into adding him in case something happened to David. Later I added Jamie so that if David couldn't take the company, she could. Jamie was my daughter. She may not have known who I was but what else was I supposed to do? I had to put her in the will. My lawyer had an updated version of the will, but I couldn't give it to David because he didn't know about Jamie.

"My lawyer suggested that Bob have a copy since he was listed as the tertiary. It made sense to put Bob in the line of succession. I should have known that Bob would try to manipulate things, like having David take the company public." Brett thought for a moment. "I've already stopped the IPO. It would have failed now anyhow.

"Bob was a skillful manipulator. Did you know that they renamed the company?" he asked. "Tashe International," he said coldly. "Tashe was Bob's mother's maiden name. I'm sure he had David agreeing to things David had no clue about. I don't know what he could have possibly told David that would make him agree to take his name off the company doors. David just wasn't ready to take over. It's my fault that all this happened."

Brett sat quietly for a moment, hung his head and added softly, "God is punishing me."

"Brett," Carol Ann began, "God is not punishing you. Bob was evil. Evil people do evil things. That's what happened."

"I'd like to believe that."

"God isn't just hanging out waiting for you to screw-up so he can punish you. He's not. He's there to help you when you stumble, when you screw up. When things get messy, he's there to help you out of it if you let him."

Brett looked her in the eyes for a moment and then turned away. "Carol," he said weakly. "I hope you're right."

"Brett," Carol Ann said, "you have the wrong idea about God. He loves you. He's not punishing you."

Brett only nodded slowly. "I don't remember you being so religious," he told her.

"I wasn't then. But bringing up a daughter as a single parent, I knew where to turn for help."

Moments passed in silence. Carol Ann looked over her shoulder at Jamie who was waiting and watching a few yards away. She reached her arm out towards Jamie and signaled her to come join them. Jamie stepped up behind them and took her mother's hand. Carol Ann looked at Brett. "Brett," she said. "I think it's time for you to meet your daughter."

Chapter 19

The man Jamie hired to tune the pipe organ in the St. James Memorial Wedding Chapel played a chord, holding it too long and too loud for Jamie's liking. She rolled her eyes upward. Phil grinned at her. They sat in the second-row pew, faced each other and craned their necks to watch the tuner as he worked in the balcony on the organ. Their conversation was constantly being interrupted as the tuner played note after note, chord after chord. This was day two of the tuning process. Jamie was glad it was almost over.

She had not noticed the pipe organ in the balcony of the church until Brett pointed it out. Brett had called and asked her to meet him at the church. Until then, she had not known that there was a balcony. The organ's pipes had been sealed into the wall when Brett had the church fixed up for Rene. It was in such need of repair and the time was so short, Brett had the contractors wall them in to make the church look nice before he gave it to her. Now the pipes gleamed of polished brass, wood and steel. The repairs had taken weeks and the tuner was the final step in the process.

There was a pause in the tuning. Phil took that moment to try and speak to her. "When's your first wedding here?" he asked.

"Next weekend," Jamie replied. "Things are booking up fast."

Jamie had accepted Brett's offer to run the wedding chapel. It was a job change and it meant moving but it was also exciting. She had never thought about how much money a building could make as a wedding venue. But she had to admit, as far as wedding chapels went, this one had to be one of the most beautiful in the country. The artwork, stained glass and intricate carvings were second to none, perhaps second to none in the world. Without advertising, word had spread about the chapel and it was being booked up rapidly.

Brett St. James walked through the open doors of the church just as the tuner played a chord. Brett froze in his tracks a moment, shook his head and began walking towards Jamie and Phil as another chord blasted through the church. He joined them, sitting in the third row behind them.

"Is he about done?" Brett asked.

"He told me about…" another organ blast, "about another half hour. That was an hour ago. He should be done any time…" blast, "any time now."

"Well, we can hear it, that's for sure." Brett said. "I think they can hear it all the way down at the restaurant."

The tuner began playing a lively tune. It sounded like a carnival song, bright and cheery. It lasted a couple of minutes. Jamie, Brett and Phil watched the tuner play from their pew seats. When he finished, he looked down, gave them a wave of his hands and said, "That's all folks."

"He must be done," Phil said with a grin.

"So," Brett began, "are you all booked up already?"

"It's booking up fast," Jamie replied. "We've got reservations with deposits as far out as June, two years from now."

"Well then," he said, grinning at the two of them. "You better make your own reservations, or you won't be able to get married in your own chapel."

Phil and Jamie both laughed.

"We're just dating," Jamie said. "Let's not rush things."

Brett looked at Phil with a grin. Phil shrugged his shoulders. Brett placed his hand on Phil's shoulders and said in a serious voice, "You have my blessing." Again, Phil and Jamie both laughed. "How about you come work for me?" Brett asked Phil. "You'll be closer."

"Uh, hi, Brett, hi Ms. Fulton," a sheepish voice interrupted from the aisleway. They turned to see Ruth Markham with her head lowered. She awkwardly held a clutch purse in front of her with two hands. Ruth and her son had stayed away from the church after the murders. It was the combination of knowing that four people had died here, including her friend, Doc, and the shame she felt for the way that she had treated Jamie. She held her eyes lowered to the floor, appearing either ashamed or afraid to look at them.

"Um, Brett, who's going to play the organ for you?" she asked timidly.

"Well, I don't know yet," Brett told her. "Jamie's running the chapel. It's her job to find someone that can play that thing." He looked at Jamie, "Any luck with that?" he asked her.

"Not yet," Jamie replied.

"Um," Ruth began. "I know how." Her voice was quiet.

"I'm sorry," Brett said. "I didn't hear you."

"I know how to play it."

"You do?" Jamie asked in surprise.

"Yeah," she said softly, her voice shaking. "I... My mom taught me to play. I used to be the organist here when this was a real church." She visibly flinched. "I mean back when we all used to go to church here." She paled and looked toward the vestibule as if looking for someplace to run.

"You still play?" Jamie asked.

She faced them again, making a weak attempt to look Jamie in the face. "I haven't played a real church organ since we closed up here, but I still play on my keyboard."

"Well," Jamie told her. "The tuner is wrapping up. It should be clear in just a few minutes. When he's done, why don't you show us what you can remember."

Ruth looked up and smiled at Jamie weakly, and then at Brett. "Thank you," she said. She looked around as if she did not know what she should say or do next. "Um," she said. "I'm just going to sit over here and wait. Is that OK?"

"Of course," Brett told her.

Ruth gave him a flinching smile, slid between the pews and sat down on the far side of the church from them. She retrieved a tissue from her purse and wiped her eyes with it. Placing her hands in her lap, she pinched the tissue between her fingers as she looked down on it with sad, unfocused eyes.

They glanced up at the tuner. He was wiping the keys one more time with a rag. He retrieved a clipboard and met them below in the main sanctuary. Brett signed off on the paperwork as Jamie and Phil shook his hand and thanked him.

All three turned to look at Ruth, who was looking at them with worried eyes. "Go check it out," Jamie encouraged. A broad smile stretched across Ruth's face as she stood and began to move more quickly. She hurried to the top of the balcony stairs and to the organ. She sat on the bench, looked over the keys and adjusted settings.

"Isn't that the woman who chased you out of here?" Phil asked Jamie.

"Yep," Jamie replied. "That's her. I wouldn't expect much here but it won't hurt to let her try."

They watched as Ruth refamiliarized herself with the organ and its settings. When she was ready, she looked down at the three of them. Her mouth was smiling with lips pinched tightly together.

"Go ahead," Jamie said with a nod, speaking loudly for Ruth to hear her in the balcony.

Ruth's smile brightened, she turned, placed her hands on the keys and began to play. The music was classical, rich and full and unexpectedly beautiful. Her playing gave Jamie the sense that they were in a much larger cathedral.

Ruth began to look as if she was hypnotized by the music. She closed her eyes and moved with a practiced smoothness, swaying gently. She and the organ became one living instrument. Her fingers glided over the keys and her feet moved across the foot pedals as if it was as normal to her as walking or breathing. Jamie was confident that Ruth knew all the names of the songs, their composers and every note by heart. The impromptu concert lasted over an hour, a concert worthy of kings and queens.

As the last song ended, she opened her eyes and looked down to see the three of them sitting on the edge of the stage looking up at her in amazed, rapt attention. She looked dazed, then flushed. Phil began to clap, and Jamie and Brett joined him as they stood, giving her a standing ovation. Tears began rolling down Ruth's face. She wiped them with a tissue, hurried down the balcony stairs and rushed out of the building. Jamie ran after her. Ruth was hired.

~The End~

Did you enjoy this book?

Thank you for taking time to read The Legacy. I appreciate it. If you enjoyed this book, would you please take just an extra moment to add a short review on Amazon? Reviews are constructive and encouraging for authors such as me.

More Books by
Ralph Nelson Willett

Available from Amazon in Paperback and Kindle Formats

The Release – Escape from Torment

After a lifetime of abuse, Carrie Rhodes escapes but now must hide from her ex-boyfriend and the gang that wants her dead. On the run and just two hours from her greatest fears in Chicago, her car breaks down. With no hope left, she resigns herself to her inevitable death.

But hope returns in the form of an extraordinary man with dark secrets and an unusual occupation. For the first time, Carrie finds herself as part of an extended family where love is unconditional and freely given.

However evil refuses to let her go and darkness rages in

many forms. Still, Carrie refuses the light that is shining in her life. Can God's love, shown through flawed people, be the path of escape from generations of torment?

The God Whistle

Mary is a busy young wife and mother whose comfortable life is shattered by one guilty and costly mistake. No one will forgive her for what happened that night and although it changed her life forever, she has no memory of it.

Desperate to save her marriage, she is led into a relationship with God through the help of a mysterious old man. Seeing how her decisions in the past have shaped her life, Mary struggles to know what God wants of her now. If she can find out, will He return her family to her? Will He give her back the life she had before the night her world fell apart?

The God Whistle is a story of faith, love, and forgiveness. With a narrative that is, by turns, emotional, mystical, warm, and dramatic, the story slowly draws the reader into its spiritual themes. It is an emotional ride from beginning to end with surprises that will keep you riveted page after page.

Want Free Books?

From time to time Ralph gives away free copies of his new releases. But his promotions are highly temporary. If you'd like to be notified when he's giving his kindle books away for free, please consider signing up at the following link: www.NorthernOvationMedia.com/freebooks

Author Contact Information
Stay In Touch

Stay in touch with the author via:

Facebook
www.Facebook.com/RalphNelsonWillett/

Twitter
www.twitter.com/northernovation

Email
AuthorRalphNelsonWillett@gmail.com

Amazon
amazon.com/author/ralphwillett